At the Speed of Light

To Tim !

Best wishes!

At the Speed of Light

Simon Morden

NEWCON
PRESS

NewCon Press
England

First published in the UK by NewCon Press
41 Wheatsheaf Road, Alconbury Weston, Cambs, PE28 4LF
January 2017

NCP 111 (limited edition hardback)
NCP 112 (softback)

10 9 8 7 6 5 4 3 2 1

ISBN:

978-1-910935-31-6 (hardback)
978-1-910935-23-3 (softback)

Cover art by Chris Moore
Cover layout by Andy Bigwood

Minor Editorial meddling by Ian Whates
Book layout by Storm Constantine

Part One:
Neutrino Dreams

1.

"Get up."

Corbyn was barely awake. He was wet; sticky gel sliding off him in thick sheets. He was covered in it, lying in it; gel was in his eyes, his ears, his nose, his mouth. He retched and coughed it plosively out over his own naked, green-tinged body. He scraped his face with his fingers, removing the remnants of the gel caul. His first breath was ragged, aching.

"Get up."

He didn't answer. Couldn't they see that he was still disorientated, unable to do anything but sit and scrape and bark and snort? The stuff clung to his eyelids, formed a net between them as he tried to see. He used his shaking fingertips to clean them.

"Get up."

He was in a tank of gel. The green came from submerged lights. As the lid had pulled up and away, the back rest had raised him to sitting. He flopped one arm out onto the side, then the other. There were other tanks around him, still closed, glowing either restful amber or sepulchral red through the viewports on the casings.

"Get up."

The voice came from the ceiling, the source hidden in the yellow-strobed darkness. Corbyn reached up and pushed the gel back from his hair and down the nape of his neck. Except he had no hair. His scalp was smooth, almost polished. When did that happen? He remembered having hair. His was sandy, short, going grey at the temples. He took another look around him. He recognised nothing.

"Get up."

Where was he? What was he doing here? He remembered his hair, but not this room. He remembered lying down and going to sleep in a bed, not a casket of slime. He surged up, suddenly active, but he slipped back, the gel sucking him down. He stared at his body. He had no genitals. He had no teeth.

"Get up."

What was this? Whose body was this? Not his. Not his own, which he knew and was comfortable in. He tried again to free himself. Slowly, carefully, he managed to push himself out and over the edge of the tub. The floor was metal, finely gridded, cold. The gel slopped off him and slowly extruded through the mesh.

"Get up."

He would if he could. These weren't his legs. They wouldn't draw up underneath him as his own did. These weren't his arms. They seemed too long. He lifted his head from the metal grid, and saw that a door, rectangular with rounded edges, had opened up in a wall. The light through there was a constant dirty white, rather than the head-pounding flash of yellow. It made it easier for him to summon the energy to drag his new-born form across the floor and over the lip of the threshold.

"Get up."

There was a table bolted to the floor, and two sets of bench seats either side, similarly fixed. Corbyn caught the edge of the nearest bench and pulled himself up. He was naked in someone else's body, and as the gel dribbled off him, it exposed more of his shock-white skin to the freezing air. His neck seemed barely able to support the weight of his skull. It kept dropping down with a jerk.

"Get –"

The ceiling squawked. Then started to rhythmically click: one beat a second, a holding pattern before it decided to speak again. Corbyn hauled his head up, let it roll around. The door had closed behind him, but he hadn't noticed until now. There was one light, positioned over the table, and that appeared to be all.

"Get dressed."

His head fell with a sudden drop. Dressed in what? He was cold, in that he could feel that he was cold, without any of the usual shivering that went with it. He inspected his arms for goosebumps, but found he was entirely hairless. This wasn't his body. This wasn't anyone's body. It was half-made, unfinished, in the shape of a man without any of the defining features.

"Get dressed."

There was still nothing to get dressed in. Something had gone wrong, and the clothes he was supposed to wear hadn't been delivered. He tried to tell the voice this. No tongue. No teeth. No lips. All that came out was a questioning bovine low. The noise terrified him: he cringed and shrank in on himself, but he had nowhere to hide. He was trapped inside the doll-like body.

"Get dressed."

He rose on unsteady legs, and started to poke around using his too-long arms. The walls were of the same construction as the floor, close-woven metal mesh, sheets and panels of it. He ran his fingers first over one wall, then another. He rediscovered the door, its opening mechanism instructed in strange pictograms. And another door, in the opposite wall, with the exact same symbols. He banged his fist against it in frustration. Where were his clothes?

"Get dressed."

This was stupid. There was nothing to wear. Surely the owner of the voice could see that? But then he heard an asthmatic wheeze from behind him, and a locker down by the foot of the wall he'd already searched popped almost open. He dug his fingers – no nails, he had no finger or toe nails, just tubes of meat and bone – he dug his fingers into the slight gap and got enough purchase to pull it the rest of the way.

"Get dressed."

Inside was a one-piece suit, blue and yellow, rubbery, close textured. If he hadn't been still slippery from the gel, he'd never have been able to put it on. A helmet, too, with a glass plate in front to see out of, and a rubber skirt about the neck. The helmet needed to go on first, with the skirt pressed against his back and shoulders to form an air-tight seal. He wrestled his head through the skirt, then clambered into the suit. It seemed too small, too tight. He felt constricted, claustrophobic.

"Get dressed."

The sound now came amplified into the helmet as well as into the room. His breathing opened and closed stops and valves, making the exhale and inhale delayed and difficult. But he was dressed. The only part of him that was exposed was his hands. He searched the locker for anything he'd missed, but there was nothing. The reflections from the one white light kept distracting him, making it seem that objects were moving just out of vision.

The ticking sound resumed. His orders were changing. Get up, get dressed, then what? He had no idea what he was, where he was, or what was expected of him. He was simply going along with the instructions because he didn't know what else to do.

"Prepare for reduced gravity."

He was in space. How could he be in space? He'd never left Earth, never spent time on an orbital, never been to the Moon. He wanted to cry out, tell the voice that there'd been a mistake, that he wasn't supposed to be there. There was nothing he could do, and he had no way of explaining himself.

"Prepare for reduced gravity."

Perhaps he should hold on to something. He turned around and took hold of the edge of the table. That didn't seem very secure, so he braced himself against the bench seat too. He waited. Some way away, deep below his feet, a noise like very heavy weights moving. He could feel the concussive vibrations through his feet, a jerk this way, a shudder that, a series of punctuated blows like a hammer rising and falling.

"Prepare for reduced gravity."

He lost contact with the deck. He tightened his grip on the table, but suddenly that wasn't enough. He was hanging from the bench: what had been a floor moments ago had now become a wall. He flailed and tried to adjust, but abruptly up and down reversed. He catapulted forward, caught his helmet on the corner of the table, and spun head-over-heels. He slammed into the wall, then slid along it as 'down' changed yet again. His feet touched down at the corner between two right-angles, then he started to drift away, back towards the middle of the room, between the table and the light.

"Prepare for reduced gravity."

How? How was he supposed to prepare for this? It was like being inside a ball, kicked at random by unseen players. He caught one foot under the table-top and tried to pull himself back towards it. The effort was too great – he was hanging by his latched foot head-first over the light. He'd crash down into it if he so much as moved. His weight increased still further. His foot began to slip. He tried to stave off the inevitable fall, his hands dangling to ward off the worst of the impact.

"Prepare for reduced gravity."

The strain in his foot lessened. It felt like the end of it, that whoever was doing whatever had finally won their contest with the controls. He floated free, moving back towards what had originally been the floor. His toes tapped the bench seat and sent him back towards the ceiling. Then the room spun around and he was falling hard. There was nothing he could do except flail his limbs as a wall, all hard unyielding metal, leapt up to break him –

2.

"So tell me, how long have you been having these dreams?"

The chair the psychologist had offered to him didn't lend itself to sitting forward, hunched over, worrying at his knuckles, but Corbyn managed it all the same. Through the slatted blinds, the sun was setting, sending orange shadows across the far wall. Navigation lights flashed from the tops of the towers, and air-cars, locked in their flight paths, glinted as they wove an aerial ballet of rising and falling.

"Mr Corbyn?"

"Sorry. I… don't know. It feels like a long time – forever – but I know that can't be true. A month. Maybe two."

He looked up and met Dr Wu Yu's forensic gaze. He felt a complete fraud, wanting to leave her consulting room at a run, and simultaneously had the urge to tell her everything, make things up even, just to please her.

"Why do you say it's only for a month? You don't seem certain."

"If it was longer, I'd remember, wouldn't I?"

"Would you? Memory is sometimes unreliable. Can you think back to a definite time before these dreams?"

"I didn't have them as a child. I'm sure of that."

Wu Yu held a finger to her lips and tapped them once, twice, three times. "The age of ten, then. Or perhaps, older, younger?"

"At least. It's only been in the last few months." He hunched over tighter, then realised the signals he was sending out. Tense. Nervous. On edge. On the edge. He purposefully uncoiled and leaned back into the chair's embrace.

"And yet, you volunteered childhood as your definite time. Not your last birthday, not New Year or other significant recent holiday. Why do you suppose that is?"

"I don't know," he said automatically. He didn't. And wasn't Wu Yu supposed to tell him?

Pre-empting his objection, she said: "We are investigating your mind, your memories, not mine. Please, try and answer the question."

"I don't know," he said again, this time conciliatory. "Can I have had these dreams for longer than I remember having them?"

"It's not impossible. The mind operates on many different levels, and only some facilitate the laying down of memories. The higher mind only remembers what is memorable. What is mundane, trivial or repetitive is forgotten almost as soon as the action is over. People can perform highly complex tasks, yet remember nothing about them the moment the task is complete."

"But dreams aren't like that, are they? Not dreams where I fall and die."

The orange glare outside deepened towards red. The reflections on the glass towers were briefly aflame before dulling to a burnt umber.

"Do you remember all you dreams?"

"No, no. Of course not."

"Then can you say that the dreams in which you do feel yourself falling and dying are more memorable?"

"Yes. That would be reasonable."

"Would you assert that those dreams are more real than the ones you don't remember?"

"More real?" Corbyn looked again at Wu Yu. He tried to hold her gaze, and failed. "More... but the other dreams are real, too, right?"

"Real in the sense that you've had them, have had to have had them, because dreams are the way the brain interprets and sorts past events. A dream you do not remember is as real as one that you do, though it barely, if at all, impinges on your conscious mind. That you are remembering these dreams, and that they reoccur, is indicative of some mental disturbance. I would like you to keep hold of the thought that you have had many, many dreams in which you do not fall and die. That these dreams are unmemorable because the dream goes, for the want of a better word, right."

"So my dreams are going wrong? Is that what you're saying?"

"There is a matter which is unresolved." She stressed that word with a pause and a turn-down in her voice. "Your dream-state – that layer of your mind which is responsible for laying down long-term memory – is raising the matter with your consciousness. Mostly, the problem solves itself. One or two disturbed nights, a feeling of discomfort or unease, and the urgency fades along with the memories of the dream. Resolution is what you seek, Mr Corbyn. The cure, such as it is, will follow quite naturally."

Corbyn nodded. That all made sense. Obviously there was something wrong in his waking life that he was having trouble reconciling. Some trauma, some suppressed trauma, was troubling him, and his awful, confusing dreams were his way of trying to sort and store those memories.

"Yes. I understand. That's perfectly clear, thank you."

"So, are you anxious about anything at the moment? Have you had a major life event, or are you anticipating one?"

"A... major life event?"

"Common stress factors: bereavement, marriage, divorce, changing or losing your job or status, impending court cases, moving house, parenthood."

"No. Nothing like that."

"What do you do, Mr Corbyn?"

"What do I do?"

"Do you have employment, private or civil? Are you a registered craftsperson or artist? Have you been appointed to local, regional or national government by ballot?"

"What do I do?" He didn't know. He didn't know what he did. He had no idea at all. He lurched forward, tense, hands on the arms of his chair, ready to spring out.

"Yes, Mr Corbyn. Is that difficult to answer?"

Difficult? It was impossible. He had no memories of doing anything except sitting down in Dr Wu Yu's long, low seat. That and... Why was he here? He had come about a dream, a dream he kept on having, night after night, but what was that dream about?

"Mr Corbyn?"

He got up abruptly. He walked to the window and held the vanes of the blind open. There was the city below, ribbons of lights threading between the buildings, and in the sky, a procession of sky cars. He had no recollection of it at all. It was as if he was seeing these things for the very first time. "Am I still dreaming?" he asked.

"That's an interesting premise. How would you go about proving that you were?"

"I can't. I don't remember anything about this, anything outside of this room." He went to the door and threw it open. There was a secretary, typing out something on a keyboard, and an empty waiting room. The man glanced up, winked conspiratorially, and went back to his work. "Who's that? Did I meet him on the way in? Did I talk to him?"

Wu Yu pushed the door closed gently, and guided Corbyn back to his seat. He perched uneasily on its very edge, while she knelt in front of him.

"You seem to be in the midst of a severe psychic episode, Mr Corbyn. Your ability to recall memories has been degraded to the point where you distrust even yourself. Trust *me*. You called and made an appointment in the usual fashion. You arrived some ten minutes early, and you sat opposite José all that time. He engaged you in conversation regarding the final game of the sportball season, which is tonight."

"Did all that really happen? Or am I just comforting myself with a dream about visiting you, trying to sort out my problems? What if, this is the dream, and the other thing isn't?"

"Can you remember the other thing now, Mr Corbyn? Can you remember what the dream was about?"

"I... was in a tank of slime. I was in a body that wasn't mine, wasn't anyone's. I tried to do something, and I couldn't because I kept on spinning around in the same room, smashing into stuff until I broke."

"And does that sound more or less likely than visiting a psychologist and talking your problems over with her?"

She had a point. But why couldn't he remember what he did, or recognise the city outside the window? Or anything at all.

He got up again and pulled the blinds up. He took hold of the handle, twisted it, and opened the window wide. The sounds of the streets echoed between the blank faces of the tall towers – a low hum, a blended buzz of machinery and voices.

"What's more real, Mr Corbyn? That, or this?"

Corbyn opened the window to its fullest extent and leaned the top half of his body over the edge. It was real. Of course it was real. As real as the strange room with the automatic voice. Just as real. He scrambled forward before Wu Yu could stop him. He was falling, head down, into the wide plaza below. He had plenty of time to wonder if Wu Yu would have tried to hold him back or talk him down, before –

3.

"Get up."

He was in a tank – a coffin-shaped tank – of slime, the consistency of shower gel. It was all over him, clinging to him like a second skin. He scrubbed and spat and shook himself free, and all the while this insistent, demanding voice kept telling him he had to get up. This stuff, this sticky, sucking, green-lit gel, had other ideas, but he eventually scrambled clear and lay, dripping, on the cold metal grid next to his tank.

"Get up."

He was the only one there, even though his tank was one of many. He used the next in line, lit from inside by amber lights, to heave himself uncertainly to his feet. Through the inspection plate in the lid, Corbyn could see a face, indistinct through the thickness of the fluid inside. They seemed asleep, perfectly still.

"Get up."

He stood, wavering, and peered around at the tanks, the different coloured lights, the regular strobing of the yellow lamp above his head. Where was he? What was he doing here? He didn't remember any of this, did he? Did he? No. Surely he didn't, because this was all new to him. These tanks, these walls, that voice.

"Get –"

The ceiling ticked at him, marking out the time, then a door opened in one of the walls. Dim white light seeped in, and he staggered his way towards it. He caught hold of the edges of the door frame to steady himself, and already he could see a body in the room beyond. It was dressed in a one piece suit, blue with yellow flashes, and a helmet over its head. There was a crack running across the wide, flat faceplate.

"Undress it. Put it in tank four."

The instruction seemed clear enough. He was being asked to strip a body, something he'd never done before. Then he had to put it into tank four, which was presumably one of the tanks behind him. How had he suddenly become the person whose job it was to strip the bodies and slide them into the waiting tanks?

"Undress it. Put it in tank four."

He stepped across the threshold, ducking down so as not to crack his head on the lintel. He noted the table and two bench seats bolted to the floor, but concentrated on the body. First, he dragged the arms so that it was no longer so crumpled against the angle of wall and floor, then straightened the legs the best he could.

"Undress it. Put it in tank four."

He pulled the long zip down from chin to crotch. The body was pale, as naked underneath as he was. The helmet had a long rubber skirt, and wouldn't come off until the suit was removed. What he needed was a knife, or a pair of scissors. What he had was his blunt, spatulate fingers. He turned the body over and peeled it like a banana. Then he wrenched the helmet free, working it loose by twisting first one way then the other.

"Undress it. Put it in tank four."

He was doing so. Surely they could see that? Now he had the body laid out, he compared it to his own hairless, sexless form. They were identical, as if there was one mould that they had both been stamped from. No ears as such, a nose that was just a ridge with a single hole, a mouth that was round, like an O rather than a crossways slit, eyes that were disturbingly human peering out from the blank slate of the face.

"Undress it. Put it in tank four."

He took hold of the wrists, cold and limp, and dragged the body to the door. Getting it over the high step was difficult. He would probably have done better turning it over so he could work with the curve of the spine rather than against it. But he managed. The feet flopped over, and he went to find tank four.

"Undress it. Put it in tank four."

Seriously? What did they think he was doing? The tanks were arranged in two rows, four on each side. The one he'd crawled from was second from the end on his right, and he inspected the lifted lid for markings. There were lots. Writing he couldn't read, symbols he couldn't interpret, and three filled circles.

"Undress it. Put it in tank four."

Why didn't they show him which one was tank four? Why did they have to make this so difficult? The tank next to his, the green-lit one with the human face in repose – and it was, a proper human face, not like his own – was marked with the same writing and the same symbols, but had one solid circle and three empty ones.

"Undress it. Put it in tank four."

That couldn't be tank four. He crossed the aisle. The lights were amber and the chamber empty. One filled circle and two empty. If he counted from the door, it was the fourth in line. It would have to do. All he needed to do now was open it. He search all around for a button or a switch, but failed to find one. Just as he was about to give up, the tank clunked, and the lid started to rise.

"Undress it. Put it in tank four."

It was going in this one, tank four or not. Corbyn pulled the body parallel to the open pool of slime, and lifted the legs into it. They slowly submerged, the entrained air making bubbles that popped and sighed. Then it was a scramble to heave the rest of it in. He got himself covered in slime, but eventually managed to arrange the body more-or-less straight in the tank.

"Undress it. Put it –"

The lid started to close automatically, and Corbyn stepped back. Tight on, the tank locked itself, and the lights winked from amber to red. Now what? He'd put the body in the tank. What else were they going to expect of him? The ceiling was ticking the seconds away, and it gave him the time to think. Where was he? Something about this place was inexplicably familiar, even though he'd swear he'd never been here before.

"Get dressed."

He knew this part. How did he know this part? He stepped back through the doorway and looked around at the bolted-down furniture and the one overhead light, the cracked helmet and the coverall. He weaved around the table and stood staring at one particular patch of the floor. Had he done this before? If so, how many times before?

"Get dressed."

He had as much difficulty getting the coverall on as he had had taking it off. The helmet was broken though: he couldn't wear that. He lifted it up to where the voice came from, tried to explain what was required in a series of bellows. No new helmet was forthcoming. What was he supposed to do? Surely they didn't expect him to put on something so obviously faulty.

"Get dressed."

Apparently they did. He squeezed his head into the opening, dealt with the rubber skirt the best he could, and stared out past the crack that ran top-right to bottom-left. Now what? He was dressed. The door to the tank room closed, sliding across the opening and then pressing itself home. The strobing yellow light was cut off, leaving him with only the single white one over the table.

"Prepare for reduced gravity."

A sudden, existential dread gripped him. He was going to die. He was going to die here, like that other misshapen thing he'd just decanted into a tank of slime, whose clothes he was now wearing, and in turn, someone else would have to scrape him off the wall and do the same to him. There was nothing he could do to prevent the whole ghastly process repeating itself.

"Prepare for reduced gravity."

He looked at the table again, even as he felt his weight ebb away. He pulled his ungainly frame over the edge of the bench seat and under the table itself. He braced himself against the supports, even though it was already a tight fit. Up and down surged and switched. He was dragged this way and that, sometimes floating, other times pressed so hard against the table legs he felt either they or he was going to snap.

"Prepare for reduced gravity."

Another savage change of direction, then a period of weightlessness that stretched on and on. He didn't dare relax his guard: the moment he did would be the moment he'd be killed. He hung on, and peered out between the bottom of the table top and the seats. A door, the one in the far end of the room, popped aside, and the ceiling ticked at him.

The scene beyond the second door was indecipherable: the light was a deep, regular pulse of red, and the occasional lightning flash of blue-white. Outside was a corridor, and that was as much as he could see. It looked chaotic, like a disaster slowly unfolding. Surely a red warning light and electrical arcing weren't a sign of all being well?

"Enter transit. Go upship."

What did that mean? Was transit the corridor outside? Upship? Which direction was that? He eased out from under the table and pushed himself towards the open door. His breath rattled the valves in the helmet, and intermittently fogged his cracked visor. He caught the edge of the doorway and peered out.

"Enter transit. Go upship."

The corridor wasn't very long, with circular doors at each end. There were two arrows painted on the walls. A black one pointing one way, a red one pointing the other. The pulsing light came from a mesh-covered cage above his head. The sparks – the sparks seemed to be appearing out of nowhere and ending arbitrarily, just torn out of the air.

"Enter transit. Go upship."

Corbyn assumed that this corridor was going to be transit, or led to it through one of the two end-doors. He manoeuvred himself through and used the ceiling handholds to pull himself forward in the direction of the black arrow. It was an even chance. The voice would tell him whether he was heading the wrong way.

"Enter transit. Go upship."

He studied the door. It didn't open for him, so he presumed

he had to do something to make it happen. Two buttons, two pictograms: an arrow pointing into an open box, an arrow pointing out. Was he already in the box? Why would no one help? Perhaps it didn't matter – but there, on the door itself, was the image of a closed box. He pressed the button with the arrow-in symbol, and listened to the chugging of machinery behind the walls.

"Enter transit. Go upship."

Was he doing this right? What if he did it wrong? Why were they sending him to do a job he was obviously unqualified for? The door slid aside to reveal a cube-shaped room, lit with strips of yellow dots, and the ghostly blue-white sparks. If this was where he was supposed to be, then he'd better get on with it.

"Enter transit. Go upship."

This was transit, then. He nudged the wall and caught the edge of the door, pulling himself in all the way and tucking his legs in behind him. The controls next to him seemed simple enough: one with an arrow, one with an empty circle. He pressed the arrow, and the door swung shut behind him. That the ceiling ticked at him told him he'd jumped through the next hoop.

The cube shuddered, and he drifted towards the door he'd entered through. The vibrations through the now-floor told him he was moving, though he had no idea where. Upship, probably. The sparks of light tearing through the air, out of nothing, into nothing, seemingly at random, fascinated him. Sometimes he got in the way – how could he not? – and the spark terminated against his rubber suit. He felt nothing: no pain, no shock, no heat. It was just something that happened.

"Exit transit. Go to core."

He was still in transit. That he hadn't moved to the other wall, and the other door on what was the ceiling, showed he was still moving. What if he was supposed to stop immediately and get out? He decided no. If he were going to the core, then he'd wait for the cube to stop. The lights glowed, the air glittered. There were odd noises and a slight buffeting, as if it was windy outside. Maybe it was. He hadn't seen outside: perhaps this really was a ship.

"Exit transit. Go to core."

He started to fall slowly towards the other door. Transit was reaching its destination. Then all motion ceased. He dabbed at the arrow-out-of-box button, and after a few moments of hissing and chugging, the door slid aside. The bright tears in the air were more a steady rain rather than the intermittent drips of before. It made it difficult to see. Some came straight at his face, striking the plate of his imperfect visor, causing him to start and blink.

"Exit transit. Go to core."

He pulled himself through and peered around the lancing light, trying to make sense of what he saw. The illumination was inconstant, flickering. Consoles that should have been bright with displays were dark and lifeless. He could feel something, too, even through the air: a juddering vibration that was almost too fast to sense. A buzzing that was more white noise than a constant note. He put his hand to the deck and there it was. It was an unhealthy, stressful sound.

The voice clicked at him. This had to be core – no, Core. This was the Core. He didn't know what that meant. The middle, perhaps, or just the most important part of where he was. Which he still didn't know. But there were big seats in front of the consoles – three of them that he could count – that had extra machinery attached to them. He drifted through the blinding lights towards them, finding that if he held his hand out over his faceplate, he could absorb the tracks before they struck his faceplate.

"Activate restart."

He had to assume that it was going to be obvious. He reached down and caught the back of one of the chairs, orientating himself so that he could sit in it. There were arms he could grip, and straps that could hold him while he worked with his hands. He lowered himself down and inspected the dead panel in front of him. Apart from a few small buttons at the base, the screen was completely blank.

"Activate restart."

If the restart wasn't here, then it'd be on one of the other consoles. He pulled himself across, and examined each in turn, but whatever he was looking for, he couldn't find it. Maybe it was something that the makers of this machine didn't want pressed by accident, only when necessary. So possibly out of the way, behind a flap or guard of some sort.

"Activate restart."

It was getting increasingly difficult to see. At first he thought this was due to his eyes, straining against the constantly-changing pattern of light and shadow, but then he realised that his helmet's visor was misting up. He couldn't clear it without taking the helmet off, and there had to be a reason why he had it on in the first place, damaged though it was.

"Activate restart."

It wasn't condensation. It was pitting. The outer surface of the transparent material was rough. His whole suit was degrading. Holes had formed, little holes joining together to form bigger ones. His forward-facing parts – chest, stomach, thighs – were like lace. It was the little streaks of light. They were picking it apart. And him. That was going to happen to him.

"Activate restart."

He'd got this far, and he didn't see any way of refusing the task. He deliberately turned his back to the direction the light was coming from, to save what was left of his sight. The restart switch had to be somewhere. He went along the back of the consoles, and there was nothing. The material they were made from was also degrading. The sparks were like a snow-storm now.

"Activate restart."

There. On the back wall. He'd never had seen it if he hadn't turned around. A square of striped colour – it was impossible to see which – and a four pointed star bursting out of an empty circle. He pushed himself towards it. As he travelled he could feel his suit peel off him: holes opening, joining, running together under tension, exposing more of his ersatz skin.

"Activate restart."

He landed next to the square, bounced slightly away. His coordination in this strange body had never been the best but now it was degrading by the moment. He spotted a handle and managed to wedge his hand under it, enough to pull him close again. His fingers were pitted, like his suit. He lifted the spring-loaded flap with his other hand. He was disintegrating, turning to dust, even as he reached forward to press the button underneath.

"Activate restart."

Corbyn felt the button push in. He could no longer hold on to the handle. The flap snapped shut, and he drifted free. The Core's consoles were lighting up on their own, flickering into life. They kept on cycling through the same sequences, trying, failing to start. They were too damaged by this hard rain of light to sustain any form of coherent function. And his body was blowing away on this actinic wind. He couldn't see, couldn't feel, couldn't –

4.

Dr Wu Yu was sitting on a little stool next to his big reclining seat, searching his face forensically for signs.

"How do you feel, Mr Corbyn?"

Corbyn blinked, looked down towards his feet. He wasn't wearing shoes, and one of his grey socks was inside out.

"What did you do?"

"I put you in a hypnotic state, so you could remember."

"And did I? Did I remember?"

He did. Snatches of it, the lights, the sparks that popped into existence like bright needles.

"You were very lucid, Mr Corbyn. In some respects, yours are classic anxiety dreams, in that you're in situations where you have no control over your surroundings, and are asked to complete impossible tasks." She looked away, out of the window. The window that he had a distinct memory of jumping from, and falling all the way down, fifty floors or more, to the broad plaza below. If he'd done that, though, then this was also a dream. He glanced at Wu Yu's profile. If he was dreaming about visiting a psychologist, then perhaps he should make use of that.

"What if they're not?" he asked. "What if this is the dream?"

Stop. Stop right there. If this is a dream, then what if the other thing was reality? A reality in which he could die and come back. Like this one. Or was he flipping from one dream to another, and back, without waking up? That would mean, sooner or later, there'd be a third place. Where he actually was. He felt a surge of panic, and gripped the sides of his chair.

"There is a condition," she said, "where the patient believes they are still dreaming when they are, in fact, awake. It's called derealisation. Is that what you think you might have?"

"But I don't think this is real either. I threw myself out of that window. That one right there. I died, and yet I'm back here. You watched me do it. What does that mean?"

"These are all very good questions, Mr Corbyn. What do you think it means?"

"I don't understand."

She folded her hands together. They were very small and slim, and the gesture very precise. "There's going to be one explanation that ties everything together. Your dreams of being in other bodies, in what you believe to be a ship, your floating and falling – a spaceship perhaps – and dying due to damage you sustain. Here, which you also believe to be a dream, sitting here, talking to me, falling to your death at your own hand."

"If these are both dreams, then I have to be asleep somewhere."

"A symptom of derealisation."

"I killed myself. I could do it again, right now." He swung his feet onto the floor and strode to the window, flinging it wide open to the cityscape beyond. Noise filtered up, the low hum that emanated from millions of people living close together.

"And where do you think you would end up? Back here? In a tank full of slime? Or somewhere else?"

"How do I wake up?"

"You open your eyes." She smiled at him. "If you are in any

form of unconscious state due to either trauma or medical intervention, it may be impossible for you to wake up. If you are normally asleep, then sufficient shock in your dreams may jolt you awake."

"Like dying, you mean." And then: "So you agree that I'm dreaming, here and now."

"I agree that you believe that you're dreaming. If you walk out of my door, you'll find a life waiting for you, a normal fulfilling life. If you jump out of my window, I can't predict where you'll end up. Dead, most likely, but if this a dream then you'll be back in your tank, with another set of tasks to perform, and you'll die carrying them out, and then you'll be here again." Wu Yu shrugged. "What do you want to happen?"

"I want to wake up. Can you help me do that?"

"I can try and prove to you that you're not dreaming, if you want."

Corbyn looked down out of the window. The plaza below called to him. "Maybe I should just do this by myself."

"I urge you not to. You came to me seeking professional advice: that is my professional advice." She rose from her stool and stood half way between the long chair and the window.

"But I won't die."

"All the evidence says otherwise – an impact with the ground from this height is usually fatal."

"I didn't die last time."

"So you say."

"But I didn't. I remember being here. I remember us talking. I remember me climbing out and falling. So yes: this is a dream, just as much as the other is, and I can't spend the rest of eternity dying in this one and dying in that one. I have to wake up somehow. If you can't help me – if the only thing you can offer me is being trapped in this better dream, then it's still being trapped in a dream. I'm sorry."

He looked out the window again, at the way the light played against the glass of the surrounding buildings, reflecting various aspects of the architecture. Then back at Wu Yu, small and neat, head bowed.

"I'm sorry too, Mr Corbyn." She reached behind her back and pulled out a slim silver gun and shot him in the chest. "Perhaps this will help."

5.

He rose from the tank with a shuddering gasp and immediately looked down. His chest – it wasn't his chest – was pale and whole and dripping with globs and sheets of gel. He was expecting a hole, just above his sternum, dead-centre, and a river of blood pouring down his abdomen. She'd shot him. Right there. He pressed his hand against his skin, and remembered.

"Get up."

She'd shot him. In reality. In a dream. He'd woken up here. Not for the first time. He scraped the gel from his eyes and gouged it out of his nose. He looked around. A yellow flashing light illuminated the room, and the two rows of tanks. The tanks were lit inside: green, amber, red. Of the eight, five were red, two were amber, and only his own was green.

"Get up."

Corbyn didn't move from his tank. He wanted to take a moment to think. He had been here before. There was the door. Beyond that door was a room, with a table and benches. Further on lay a corridor, and more doors, and little needles of light that winked in and out of existence. He'd done what the voice had told him. It had always ended in failure.

"Get up."

It had always ended with him back in a sunlit room, high up in a city tower. Just him, and a woman, talking. Him telling her about this place. Her trying to interpret his dreams. Together, trying to make sense of them. She'd called this series of rooms a spaceship. He looked again. It could be. There were enough clues. The tanks. The variable gravity. The direction upship. The consoles. The chairs.

"Get up."

Why was he on a spaceship? Why was he dreaming he was on a spaceship? The two questions seemed interchangeable, and less significant than the fact that he was being asked to crew it, to fix things, to save it from destruction. The tanks contained his previous attempts, except the last one, where there was nothing left to retrieve. The sparks of light had chipped the flesh from his bones and turned those bones to dust.

"Get up."

The voice was always telling him to get up, to get dressed, to go through this door, to go through that door. The voice was always leading him to an inevitable death. So, the obvious solution was for him to ignore the voice. Do something different. Something unexpected. The amber tanks contained unfinished meat puppets, disposable skin suits which could be controlled by… How? Implanting consciousness? That was how they were supposed to work, but he was the ghost in the machine. He shouldn't be here.

"Get up."

This: this wasn't his ship. He had his own. That was it. He had his own spaceship, a different design, a different purpose. Somewhere, out beyond the metal walls, that was where he truly existed. But right now he resided here, inside this body, sitting up in a tank of gel, trying to save this ship instead. Where was the actual crew? He needed not to get up, but get them up. He eased himself out of the sucking gel, sloughing it off back into the tank as he stood.

"Get up."

He was going to do what he wanted from now on. Even if this was only a dream, in the same way that the room in the tower was a dream, he didn't just have to follow instructions. One amber tank held a clone of himself. The other was different. He knelt down next to it and peered through the inspection plate. Her face was complete, finished, and peaceful in repose, unaware of the disaster unfolding around her.

"Get up."

He searched the carapace for an opening mechanism. Before – when he'd had to put the broken body into an empty tank – the whole process had been automatic. But there had to be a manual override. And yet, he found nothing on the first sweep. None of the symbols helped, and what he presumed to be writing was impenetrable.

The ceiling clicked. The voice, and whatever sensors were attached to it, had finally noticed that he was walking around. He made another pass over the outside of the tank, probing and poking, seeing if anything pushed down or popped up. Nothing. He tried to sit back on his haunches, slipped in a pool of gel, and fell back against the wall.

The door at the far end of the room slid aside. White light filtered through, fighting against the flashing yellow. He could see part of the table, the edge of the bench seats. Just as he remembered.

"Get dressed."

He inspected the ends of the tank. They were as smooth and featureless as the rest of it. So, what was he going to do? He gazed at his blunt fingers, so singularly unsuited for forcing an entry. There had to be a way to open the tank without relying on the automatic systems. It was just well-hidden. Away from the tanks themselves, perhaps. A control board. He looked up at the wall he was leaning against, then clambered to his feet.

"Get dressed."

He banged his fist over the panelwork, and something gave. He traced the outline of a rectangle, and pushed at the corners one by one, then two by two. Finally he found the right combination, and the edge of the panel became proud of the surface. He dragged his fingers against it, and gained enough purchase to pull it open.

"Get dressed."

This was what he wanted. He moved down the selection until he found one filled circle, three empty ones, right at the bottom. There was a series of four tell-tales, all lit amber, and a rotating switch. It was pointing to his right, to the closed box. On the opposite side was an open box. That was clear enough. He hoped it wouldn't kill her.

"Get dressed."

He turned the switch. There was considerable resistance to the movement. But when he got halfway, it snapped round, and things started to happen. The first tell-tale winked green. He crouched down by the tank and watched the face through the inspection plate for signs of distress. At the second green light, the muscle ticks started, and by the third, her whole body was shivering. He didn't know if this was good or bad.

"Get dressed."

On the fourth green light, a motor kicked in. The tank casing split in two and the top began to rise. Gel spilled out through the widening crack, and her head and torso started to angle up into the air. He reached out, and hesitantly pushed the gel away from her mouth. She seemed to have stopped shivering, and now looked slack-faced, asleep.

"Get dressed."

Suddenly, her eyes opened. Her mouth did too – he could see her white teeth and her pink tongue – and she inhaled strands of sticky mucus, coughing it out hoarsely on the next breath. Her flailing hands came up to grip the sides of the tank, better to brace herself for the next haul of air. He didn't know what to do now to help. He recalled his own struggles with the gel, and guessed that everyone had their own way of dealing with it.

"Get up. Get dressed."

The wind whistled inside her lungs. Her fingers cleared her eyes and nose, and she dragged her hands over her face, leaning forward, panting. Her head, with its fine coating of matted black hair, shone under the sweep of the yellow light. Then she straightened up, and saw Corbyn crouched by her side.

"Get up. Get dressed."

She looked straight at him, and obviously she didn't see Corbyn: she saw one of the meat puppets. She turned her head all around to see who else was waking. When she realised the answer was no one, she turned back to him, frowning hard. She spoke breathlessly to him: nothing but a meaningless stream of phonemes, human sounds stitched together in an entirely unfamiliar pattern. Yet he could understand her as clearly as he could the voice.

"Have we reached our target? Why haven't the other units been activated?"

"Get up. Get dressed."

She glanced up. "Control: status."

The ceiling clicked. Corbyn moved back from the woman, afraid of her completeness, her ability. He was just some lumpen golem, while she was fearfully and wonderfully made. Her face contorted in discomfort as she drew her legs up and lifted them one at a time over the edge of the tank and onto the floor. She spoke to him again.

"What's your installation?"

And when he didn't answer immediately, she said quickly:

"Are you malfunctioning?"

He lowed at her, beast-like. There was nothing else he could do, no way he could communicate.

"Control: status."

The ceiling kept on ticking. It had nothing to say, either.

She got to her feet, glistening, beautiful, and looked under his lowered head, because he had to turn away.

"What's your installation? Why don't you respond? Control? Status?"

He shied away again, dodging past her the best he could and heading for the door and the light beyond. He stopped when he got there, because he could see the first intimation of blue-white needle-thin streaks drawing themselves in the air. There was nothing he could do any more. If the sparks had reached this far, there'd be no entering Transit, no upship ride to the Core. He'd fall apart before he'd reach even half-way.

"Where are you going? Control?"

He turned to apologise in the only way he could, and stepped backwards through the door. The door closed between them, shutting her off in that last refuge, and him on the other side. The last he saw of her was her striding towards him on quickening feet, trying to get to him, reaching out her hand, then snatching it back when she realised that she wouldn't make it.

He'd failed. He hadn't saved her after all, hadn't saved the ship. It was breaking down around them, and it would soon fall apart completely, eroded away by the light. All the cycles of dying and rebirth had been in vain. He felt the first predations of the sparks against his back. He rested his head on the door, as it was the closest he could be to another living being as he waited for his disintegration.

But wait: there was something important he needed to consider. He wasn't a living being at all, not like her. He wasn't flesh and blood, but the vital animating spirit in a complex web of circuitry and sensors. His shoulders sagged. If this was a dream, then he was dreaming of a life he could never have. How bittersweet, how poignant, that he should experience even death, when all he had was an off-switch. How he remembered everything –

Part Two:
Beam Rider

1.

Corbyn slowly became aware of the ship. It had been built around him so that he'd run it in the same way a human mind would run a body – most of the time, entirely without conscious thought or effort. His nerves and muscles ran not down limbs but struts and channels. His endocrine system was a thousand different tell-tales, constantly recording and reporting back, carrying messages and making tiny adjustments. If he had blood, it came in the stream of electrons that surged from the furnace of his heart to every extremity. His self-knowledge was such that he could reach in and alter anything, simply if it didn't feel right.

How then, had he fallen asleep? That had never been part of the mission. It wasn't even part of his parameters. No one had ever said, 'and at some point you will fall asleep'. A search through his documentation – voluminous and detailed – had references to sleep mode, when an automatic sensor could be rested while still being triggered by a pre-defined range of stimuli. Others cross-referenced hibernation, things he could deliberately put into storage because they weren't needed during that part of the voyage.

But sleep? He didn't need sleep. He never grew tired. He didn't accumulate toxins. He didn't need to move memories from short-term to long-term. Stored by the plastic connections within a semi-crystalline matrix, everything he was lay deep behind layers of physical and electromagnetic shielding. Sleep was for organics.

Time had unequivocally passed. He checked. He checked

again, knowing that there couldn't possibly be any mistake, but checking anyway, drilling down through the layers of data that that accumulated in their buffers while he was... what? He couldn't call it off-line. He wasn't. Everything had carried on running: the automatics had kept working, the systems had been maintained, the course...

The course. He had telescopes, wide-field viewers, dishes and antennae. An artificial mind such as his should be immune to panic. Panic was a chemically-induced reflex, and he had none of the hormones and none of the receptors. Yet as he peered outside, he could feel – they'd built him to feel – fear.

He scanned the visual spectrum first. Stars were bright, their positions and spectra known. He could identify them and fix his position in space. He ran the diagnostics because nothing seemed to be working. He turned on the inspection lights down the entire length of the ship, and he could see it perfectly. The base of the flaring cone ahead, the spherical tanks tucked in behind, the long stem leading to the reactor, the exhaust bell behind. The faint glow of his wake. It was his equivalent of looking in a mirror. He'd checked himself out and he looked in pretty good shape.

But where were the stars? There was nothing behind. There was an indistinct halo girdling him, tiny points of light on an exact circle, orthogonal to his travel. They winked in, then out, of view. Ahead was a diffuse white disk. That was it. That was all he could see. Except... Except. There was something else. Not as close as his superstructure. Not as far as infinity. He aimed his centimetre dish and pinged it. A thousand kilometres away, matching vectors. His optics weren't designed for that range of focus, but he could fix that with an algorithm.

It looked as if part of his own ship had broken off and was drifting. It wasn't, though. He had no missing mass, no severed nerves or inoperable controls. The object gave no light of its own, but displayed a scattered blue glow on the leading edge. He interrogated the object further: illuminating it with a microwave laser and reading the reflections. Two kilometres long; at most, fifteen metres wide. A slim, open structure, apart from a mass at the front, something halfway down, and a big trailing end. Another ship. Not a design he recognised, because he passed its silhouette across all the known varieties and came up with nothing, but theoretically, yes. The large mass at the back was the drive, the midsection was probably control, the forward part the shield.

He probed the area around it. The drive was off. The shield seemed purely matter, and very little of it at that. The blue-white Cherenkov light glowed hard around it. He scanned the usual radio frequencies, running from centimetre to kilometre lengths, and there was nothing active, only passive radiation. It was dead. A derelict. A ship that coincidentally shared the same vector as him, wherever he was.

Even without doing the calculations, Corbyn knew this was on the outer curve of coincidence. Space was empty and very big. The chances of two ships sharing the same part of it, coincidentally, were vanishingly small. Given that, the only explanation was that this other ship was there because he was, matching his velocity and his direction until it could come alongside.

It had done that. Just. The sheer effort of doing so had caused it to fail. He still might be able to learn something, though. If he made a subtle change in his drive, he could be alongside in less than an hour. His ship wasn't made for manoeuvrability. It steered, as one of his makers had joked, like a cow. He looked at an image of a cow, standing on four legs, chewing repetitively. He could use idiom, but not necessarily understand it.

He could stand off the other ship. Ten kilometres was a safe distance, and he could cover it with his electromagnetic scoop, sheltering it from the oncoming wind of particles. Perhaps some of the remote systems on it were still operational, and he could interrogate them. He might find out why the ship was following him.

2.

Corbyn couldn't deny the truth any longer. He was nowhere he expected to be. And he was moving faster than he thought possible. He'd fallen asleep with his foot on the throttle. For ten years. For all that time, his scoops had been wide open, catching interstellar hydrogen and funnelling it into his reactor, to be fused together and thrown out behind him in a continuous explosion of heat and light.

He had accelerated from a perfectly acceptable half c to something – he hated estimating, but his instruments simply weren't precise enough to calculate the exact number – close to c. Very close to c. His best guess was that he was travelling, subjectively, at nine hundred, ninety-nine thousand, nine hundred and ninety-five millionths of the speed of light. That numinous disc in front of him was the echo of the creation of the universe, blue-shifted all the way to visible.

He had, of course, immediately throttled back at that point, running the reactor at the level required to maintain enough power to run the ship, but nothing more. He reined in his scoops, too, so as to not collect so much hydrogen. If he turned them off, he'd end up like the derelict. Disintegrating in a blue corona.

He had a decade of images to review, a decade of data. And if ten years hadn't seemed much to start with, that was only ship time. The civilisation that had launched him was now, conservatively, dead. It was fifteen hundred years older than when he'd left it. Corbyn knew his history – all of it, he had an overview of everything from the Palaeolithic onwards – and he knew that cultures rose and fell, because they were human.

His primary target lay light years behind. He'd simply failed to decelerate at the half-way mark and had gone sailing by, three ship-years into the voyage. He couldn't so much as see that star. Its light had been shifted so hard into the longer wavelengths, he had nothing suitable with which to pick up its faint radio signals.

All the stars in his immediate navigation map were behind him, and invisible.

He was left with the distant, fixed stars which, because of the distance he'd travelled, had shifted. The stars passing through the halo that marked his midline, whose light was shifted neither blueward or redward, were simply stars. If they had significance, that detail was lost to him. He measured their spectra while he could, but without any parallax for distance he had no clue as to which of the lines in his catalogue they might refer.

He could calculate his travel through space-time, though. A thousand light years, roughly in the direction of the plane of the galaxy and spinwise. Enough to take him to the edge of the spiral arm, if not beyond. His course probably wasn't straight. How not straight depended on how close to gravity wells he'd gone. He could make use of the visual data he'd collected to work that out. Space was empty, but his initial encounter with his target star would have warped his trajectory, a little at least, and after that, who knew?

He took a moment to watch the progress of the derelict. Surely, his makers wouldn't have sent something after him? And if they had, how did they think they could find him? That idea was so unlikely as to be easily discarded. Yet this ship had destroyed itself in an effort to intercept him. Salvage? Had they hoped to hijack his systems, slow him down, turn him around, take him somewhere and break him up?

That wasn't the answer, either. Even if successful, the ships would be gone for centuries. Decelerating from near light-speed would take at least a year or two, and all the while, the clock would be running fast. Initially, very fast. He had to admit that he didn't know why the other ship was there. He would try and get answers: now that the derelict had stopped being degraded by relativistic particles, he had time.

3.

Why had he fallen asleep? That he had was undeniable. He had the data to prove it. He was a machine. A construct. He should have stayed awake for the whole, subjective, voyage. He should have turned over halfway. He should have gone into orbit around the primary target, and transmitted data on the planetary bodies that had been detected there. After a few years, when all his mission parameters had been met, he'd move on to the next star on his list.

It wasn't as if they'd only made one of him. They knew what they were doing. By the time they'd bolted his ship together and imbued the matrix with intelligence, it was almost routine for them. He knew the history of the programme. That early disasters had gradually turned into triumphs. That the first message had been beamed back to Earth from another star twenty years before his launch. That his design was proven. Tried and tested.

He conceded that malfunction was the most likely explanation, even though all his systems remained nominal. That left him suspecting his own mind, and he had no way of diagnosing his own faults. If there was a structural problem, a flaw in the substance that held his mind, he couldn't repair it anyway. If it was deeper, psychological, then his reality had already altered, and he would perceive that as normal.

But sleep? That was an extraordinary frailty to develop. His makers had elided the difficulties of training a mind, and very much downplayed the outcomes for an aberrant artificial intelligence. Depression, psychosis, schizophrenia, OCD – that was apparently quite common, so his makers said – mania: the list was comparable to that for humans. Sleep was not an illness, though. It was a feature of a biological brain, something he clearly didn't have.

He went back to the start of his mission, and looked for key indicators of awareness. He realised that he might not be able to spot a sleep-state, as such, but if he could find signs of inattention, then he might be able to document his transition. Data was continually received by his many instruments, feeding back automatically according to prewritten algorithms. That would happen whatever: even if his mind became so corrupt it no longer functioned, the ship's systems would still work.

In that event, however, if he was unable or unwilling to deal with alerts or alarms, the ship would fail safe. The reactor would idle. His consciousness would be polled regularly. If he didn't respond, he would be turned off, and the ship itself would attempt to park around a star, somewhere, anywhere. He had evidently avoided that fate. He had passed all the tests, for ten years, while being completely unaware of doing them.

That, at least, was something to report back, if he ever could, and there was anyone to report back to. His makers would be dead. Their descendants might be living in caves. There was an even chance of that. He wondered if they told stories of that time, when they sent probes to other stars, to explore far beyond where they would ever travel. His makers put a great deal of effort into the programme. It would be a loss if none of them were remembered.

How would they remember him, though? The one that failed, that powered away on a spear of light, never to be heard of again. The one they listened for, hoping, waiting, then giving up on. The one that was lost. There was a story about a man, a sea captain in the age of sail – Vanderdecken – who, in some versions cursed his god and in others his devil, and thereafter was condemned never to reach port. Corbyn was Vanderdecken, and any ports he might call home were a thousand years in the past.

This ship, though, this derelict, had to come from somewhere. All this time, he'd assumed that this was a human-built artefact, just like him. That didn't necessarily follow. Interesting. He opened up the First Contact protocols and ran through the flowchart. Most of the decision boxes, whichever way he went, ended with him in the Initiate Self Destruct Sequence oval. So far, he was safe. He'd scanned the ship, hailed it, and determined that it didn't pose an immediate threat.

And, of course, the people who wrote the protocol had long gone. The flowchart was now more of a suggestion than a set of iron rules. He felt the urge to adhere to them to the letter, but the rationale to do so was weak. He could make his own choices. He could make all his own choices, regarding everything: there was a weight to that decision, a heft he needed to wield cautiously.

He'd slept. While he'd slept, he'd run his systems perfectly. He'd dealt with all the alarms, all the alerts, all the routine maintenance he'd needed to check through. That didn't seem possible. His makers once used a phrase, and he could look it up and check its meaning, about being in the zone. Corbyn had understood it baldly to mean doing things right, first time, but as he examined his data, he wondered.

Not sleep. Flow. Not an unconscious state where he was aware of nothing, but a hyper-alert state where he was aware of everything, reacting in a split-second, all the information pouring in and feedback pouring out, just as he'd been trained to do. Except none of that had impinged on his higher functions. While his reflexes dealt with the routines, he'd entered a trance-like disassociative fugue. He'd accelerated out of the solar system. He'd kept on accelerating.

He'd got up to his cruising speed of half c. He should have throttled back at that point, opened the pinch-point in his reactor, and let the hydrogen heat up enough to provide electricity without it fusing into helium. The speed of his reactions was such that perhaps he thought he was going slower than he really was. He passed point six, point seven, and whatever was going on outside, the universe compressing down, the light ahead of him shifting to blue, behind him to red and infrared, he just sucked up more and more hydrogen, at higher and higher energies. The rate of his acceleration in his own inertial frame remained fairly constant. Outside it, though, he was going faster, faster.

He'd hit point nine c. Then point nine nine c. His relativistic mass increased exponentially, as did his energy, but the faster he went the more hydrogen his wide-open scoops shovelled in from the greater volume of space he passed through. His velocity increased. He was currently travelling at a trivial one kilometre a second below the speed of light, though he'd never close that gap.

Something had stopped his flow, and had brought him to his senses. Literally. Something that his reflexes couldn't deal with. The appearance of the other ship off his side? That was likely. He wasn't pre-programmed for that scenario. The other ship had caught him up and appeared out of the blur of darkness behind him. His sensors had found it, and not been able to parse it. Now he was doubly intrigued. This mystery ship had saved him from driving blindly on until he crossed the galaxy and out the other side. A pity it had destroyed itself doing so.

4.

He was armed with a full array of imaging equipment, but his optics were optimised for planetary sensing in the tens of thousands of kilometre range. He could, however, rewrite much of his software, and he wasn't restricted to visible light. He could see just as well in radio waves and the infrared, even if the resolution wasn't so sharp.

He could do things with his laser, too. Either he could perform a millimetre by millimetre scan of the derelict to build up a virtual model of it in his memory, or he could pump it with power and burn holes in what was left of its hull. That was one of the reasons he was content to let the other ship get close to him. A messaging laser designed to send a signal over light years was a lethal weapon close-quarters. That, and his drive: a highly-radioactive billion-degree exhaust plume that would act like a directable solar flare.

Odd that his thoughts turned to defence options rather than the course of action mandated on the First Contact protocols. The authors of that document were anxious that any entity representing Earth didn't appear aggressive, choosing suicide and a thorough obliteration of information over retaliation every time. There was no point in the flowchart where the decision box allowed him an active response.

His individual needs were necessarily subordinate to the mass of humanity, the billions that he had left behind. All the probes that they'd sent out had exactly the same set of orders: if you encounter other life forms, learn what you can, as safely as you can. If there is a chance of you, your ship, your data, being compromised, delete everything and scuttle your ship. Do not, under any circumstances, think you know better.

And here he was: Corbyn, thinking he knew better. There was a word for this: hubris. It had been said, in conjunction with the place of hubris in ancient Greek plays, that those the gods wished to destroy, they first made mad. He needed to be higher minded. Self-sacrifice was a noble end. But if he was careful…? He was already sliding conditionals into the certainty of the protocols, and had to acknowledge that killing himself would feel just like killing himself. It was no different for him than it would be for a human. It was supposed to be difficult, and the needless throwing away of life was societally disruptive.

Out here, though, further than anyone or anything had ever gone, as far away from any concept of home as it was possible to get, displaced in both time and space, he was on his own, and was possibly the last of his kind. Of any kind, for that matter. Humanity could be gone. Why did they give him the capacity to make decisions if they only wanted him to make the decisions they wanted? They could have sent a robot. Instead they sent him.

He finished making the virtual model of the derelict. There

were assumptions needed, of course. He couldn't see around it, so he just filled that in blank. What he *could* see was telling. The ship was the shape of a long, lattice-work spine, the systems bolted on to it. The drive at the stern wasn't cold, but it was cooling. The emissions were… difficult to interpret. That this ship worked at very high energies was obvious, because how would it have otherwise caught up with him, but its actual mode of producing that energy was opaque.

The long open section between the drive and the next set of modules was well-preserved, much better than the corroded upper section. Even with the drive intact, the forward part of the ship would never survive acceleration. From what he could see, there were tracks inside the structure, and at the back of the mid-section, something that might conceivably move up and down those tracks. Of course, he didn't have anything like that, because he didn't need it. Something like that would only be required if –

If there was a crew. If there was a crew who had to move backwards and forwards to the drive to maintain it. That meant that the mid-section had to be crew quarters. He called up the old plans of ships that carried humans, to see the comparisons. Air-tight chambers. Breathing gases. Liquid water. A centrifuge. Storage. Venting. Hydroponics. What he was looking at should be bigger if intended to accommodate crew. Yet it was built into the design, the most obvious of which was the distance between the drive and the mid-section. Why do that if you weren't trying to protect the organics from whatever toxic particles the drive spat out?

Looking towards the bow, the structures were severely degraded. Whatever had been there was now open to space. Remnants of some solid, dense material, shielding he presumed, was still clinging on, but it had almost completely evaporated. Even in interstellar space, there was always something to run into. He had vast electromagnetic fields to capture and control such particles. Otherwise driving into them at nearly light-speed would result in what he was seeing now.

Just below the ruin of the forward section was a capsule, wedged in the lattice spine. It looked identical to the one at the back of the midsection. Whoever had been in it was now no more than molecules smeared out over a million kilometres of space. Had they known their ship was disintegrating? Had they done everything they could to save it? Not that it mattered: the design was flawed from the start, and would always eventually fail. Not like him. He could keep going until the end of time itself.

There were no signs of anything useful coming from the forward section. He examined his image of the midsection modules. They seemed a strange collection of spheres and tubes, put together, if not hastily, then with a more utilitarian bent than his own designers. He was almost elegant in comparison. The chief thing that struck him again and again was the small amount of living room. Perhaps the occupants didn't need as much as humans. That they didn't would certainly mark them out as alien.

The leading edges of the modules were heavily scarred, but when he went looking for them, he could find no traces of breathable gasses. The pressure vessels were intact. They were warmer than the surrounding space, which might show that power had failed only recently. There were even vague radio sources inside, showing that some sections may still be running off batteries. Life support ought to be the last thing to go. Cruel, always, but basic psychology: the most vital functions would be the ones conserved the longest.

Did that mean that there was something still alive in there? If so, could he help them? He didn't have any pressurised areas himself, let alone any of the things to keep someone alive, whatever their biology. He had maintenance bots he could deploy outside his hull. He might be able to reroute some of his power to the modules, and keep them functioning for longer. He could try and talk to whoever was inside. Ask them what they wanted him to do.

Was he lonely? Was that it? Had he entered the flow, and

stayed there for ten years, because he had nothing to keep him engaged? He'd enjoyed talking to his makers. He'd listen to their conversations, even and especially when they weren't specifically addressing him, and was charmed – was that the right word? – by the interplay between them. He'd been alone, but he'd been built to be alone. And after all that time, he found that he craved company.

How would he do it? The derelict was longer than his ship, and bringing alongside and necessarily in contact would be impossible. He could cut out the midsection, burning through the lattice fore and aft with his laser, try and nudge those parts away, and close on what was left. If it crashed into him, then something vital might break. He might be able to fabricate a skeleton framework on his hull to better catch the modules, absorb most of the impact and perhaps even stop it bouncing away.

Some of his bots could hang on while others tied it on. It wouldn't be a permanent solution, but it might be enough. There were probably a dozen better ideas, but they'd take longer to achieve. Time was now the critical factor. He wasn't to endanger himself: not recklessly, anyway. He certainly wouldn't be self-destructing, no matter what the protocols said. He showed his bots what he wanted, and slavishly they scuttled out onto the hull to make it. They were really part of him, his systems, his sensors, but he saw them as one step removed from him. There was no harm in that.

He spent some moments checking vectors, wondering if he could actually do this, or he was simply going to cause a disaster that once started, couldn't be avoided. Then he did it anyway. He was a thousand years in his own future, and saw no good reason not to.

5.

He didn't want to apply any torque to the derelict. Their relative speeds were exact, but he had no way to stop the midsection modules from spinning once they'd started. He'd have to cut very carefully, even though he was using only light. Expanding plasmas exerted a pressure, and he couldn't cut evenly all the way around. He'd have to heat up the connecting latticework from one side only. That was going to produce a turning force.

Counter-acting that force, by applying exactly the same pressure on the other side of the midsection was really the only option. He didn't know where the centre of mass was, though. Finding it was the solution. Somewhere between the midsection and the drive would be a point where he could burn through, and produce little torque, or even none at all if he got it right. An impulse at the centre of mass would affect the whole structure, moving it away from him. With a tight, even cut, he'd separate the drive: he could then push it clear using the same effect he needed to avoid. Millisecond bursts would sputter the outside of the drive mechanism, causing tiny explosions and fast-moving clouds of vaporised material. Every action still had an equal and opposite reaction. He could steer that segment away.

Then he could do the same for the fore section, though the new centre of mass would lie very close to the modules he was trying to save. Push that back. Then try and shave off the excess superstructure on the aft side, probably the most difficult cut of all. The mass of the object would be much reduced, and his laser's effect much greater.

It was ironic, considering that the relativistic mass of the ship was vast, and the energy it represented enormous. Because he shared the same reference frame, none of that mattered. An outside observer would see two flat discs of matter weighing – in Corbyn's case at least – tens of millions of tonnes, edging with glacial slowness towards each other over a period of weeks, while he was worried something might happen too quickly for him to be able to correct it.

He focussed his centimetre radar on the derelict, and worked out the rate of approach at several points along its length. All the values added up. He set that routine to run automatically and flag him when it changed. Then he powered up the laser, guessed using simple geometry and material science where the centre of mass was, and flicked a microsecond burst of light to strike the latticework. His optical cameras peered into the puff of vapour given off, and examined the spectra of the tiny cloud as it cooled and dispersed.

Not metal, then. Silicon and carbon, mainly. Fibreglass of some sort. He checked how well the structure conducted heat, with some well-timed bursts from the laser and his infrared detector. The answer was not very, which counted in his favour. The part of the structure he was aiming at would heat up quickly, and break down faster as a result. If it had been superconducting, he would have been totally thwarted.

He dug down, burning and measuring, adjusting his target as the data came back. He zeroed in on the centre of mass and started cutting in earnest, his laser chewing its way through the first strut on the lattice without incident. He waited for the vapour to disperse properly, and checked everything again. So far, so good. He had another seven struts to sever, and the ones on the far side were going to be difficult. He probably ought to cut a larger section out of the front of the lattice to access the rear.

He mapped out his surgery again, and set to. He had almost doubled the number of pieces to laser his way through, and the ship was getting closer all the time. It was now fifty kilometres distant, and his planet-sensing optics were being tested to their limit. He should back off a little, but there was always the module's battery life to consider. Outside his hull, his bots were sintering together a scaffold to hold the midsection. They were about halfway through, and would be finished long before he was.

As far as he could tell, he'd cut a wedge from the lattice just ahead of the drive section. He pulsed his laser at one edge of it, and yes, it floated free, driven from its hole on an exhaust of plasma. He watched it drift for a moment, calculating trajectories and making sure that wasn't going to interfere with anything he would subsequently do. He sliced through the remaining three struts at the back, and the only thing holding the two sections together now was some ducting. It shattered when he hit it, shards of the casing spinning out and away. He could just about see them before they blurred and vanished. Each piece was too small to cause problems. Everything was nominal.

He nudged the drive out. He didn't have to worry about nuance or fine control for this part. He pushed it back and away, giving it a delta of a few centimetres a second. It was enough. He added the trajectory to the map he was building up, and ran it forward and backwards through subjective time. No collisions predicted. Now for the remains of the fore section.

He probed and tested, then cut out another wedge, exposing the back of the lattice. He was prepared for the ducting this time, dialling down on the power and melting rather than breaking it. He nudged the structure away: much less to aim at this time, but still plenty. He sent this section slowly spinning into the black void, where it would eventually leave the protection of his scoop fields and become exposed to the relativistic wind.

One more series of cuts, close to the aft of the modules, was complicated by the capsule still docked there. He could deal with that if it got loose, if he had enough time. Too close, and he may not be able to evade if it came his way. He concluded that he needed to neutralise that threat first, by locking the capsule in place. The lattice that contained it didn't seem conducive to buckling: perhaps aiming for the capsule itself would be better.

First things: having done this twice already, he was confident that cutting the lattice stem again wasn't going to cause unexpected problems. He started on making the wedge shape, while examining the cylindrical capsule. The derelict was close enough now that he could use his short focus hull cameras to image it, albeit imperfectly. It had entered the range where he was distinctly myopic. He wasn't comfortable about that.

He went back to his model. The capsule was parked against the modules, and presumably held by clamps. Only if he did something unexpected would he shake it loose, and he wasn't planning on doing that. It was a risk, depending on what could be a dead, automatic system that might fail open than fail safe, but there were enough unknown variables to make him think that the only viable option was to simply do nothing. He could meddle, and make things worse in an unpredictable way. Or he could leave it alone.

He checked that he had enough space against him to accommodate the extra length. He did, though, find that he'd have to extend the superstructure he was building outside. He gave his bots the new parameters and told them to get on with it. He'd cut the wedge. He checked the distance again, found it was thirty-five kilometres, and made sure that there was no rotation. Everything was going according to plan. He was safe. The midsection was safe. The parts of the derelict he'd cut off were moving away at already-determined vectors that weren't going to cross.

He wondered what his makers would think of all this? He hoped they would admire his technical competence and patience. Perhaps it would in part make up for his failure to carry out his mission. He was expensive – a considerable amount of resources was put into the programme as a whole, and each ship represented a sizeable investment that could have been directed elsewhere. There was – there had been – still poverty and deprivation on Earth, though not comparable to former times in history. If it hadn't been a relative golden age, he'd never have been built. His makers had had the time and luxury to look up to the stars, rather than concern themselves with mere survival.

He had no way of knowing if this was First Contact. He'd been lost to history for millennia. But he was still a very long way from Earth, and there was no chance of any other human-made artefact being this far out. Even if this wasn't *the* First Contact, it was likely to be *a* First Contact. He wondered what they looked like. He could make some assumptions from the way they built their spaceship, but it didn't help much.

Not that it mattered what they looked like. He – Corbyn – wasn't one to judge the worth of a mind based on the body that housed it. His own was nearly a kilometre long and had a rest mass of a hundred thousand tonnes. There were theories that everything should look vaguely humanoid. Those theories might be hopelessly wrong. He could shortly be in a position to find out.

How was he doing? The midsection modules were thirty kilometres distant. He had accurate measurements of them and knew how quickly they were moving towards him. He was confident he could catch them and secure them against his own hull. He'd then be in a position to identify the electrical feed or feeds, and wire them into his own system. Guessing at the current and voltages, the phases and cycles, was going to be harder work. Bringing any automatic systems on line harder still. The portions of the derelict he'd separated off were slowly moving away. The larger fragments, the drive and fore-section, were slower than the smaller pieces of the lattice, but nothing intersected.

There was nothing to do now but wait. He didn't mind. Waiting was part of him.

6.

Had he found his flaw, his inherent weakness that had allowed him to lose ten years of ship-time? It was while he was watching the numbers representing the distance between him and the midsection, that he found himself more fascinated by the tumbling digits than what the digits represented. He felt his conscious mind starting to drift, caught up in the simple linear regression, anticipating the next, smaller value and feeling satisfaction when it appeared.

As he slowly, inexorably, fell towards a trance, he was aware of watching himself do it. He deliberately looked away from the numbers, and with his attention now not fixed on the flickering, photic drive, he felt himself return to normal. This happened in human brains, affected by strobing lights, inducing a form of disassociation. He had it too. The modules were a kilometre distant. His last conscious thought had been when they were four kilometres out.

He was built to watch numbers. He'd passed all his tests pre-launch tests, and had piloted his ship out of the solar system perfectly. He must have developed the tendency later on. Something in his crystalline mind had changed, a series of connections that had led to the formation of unhelpful pathways. It was problematic that he suffered from this abnormality, but now that he knew about the condition, he could put mechanisms in place to stop it happening again. Especially now. He was so close.

He deliberately introduced routines that would sound random bursts of music – atonal, and nothing with a repeated pattern – into his feed. He used the value of pi, and assigned each value a note. A four note bar would play, again at random intervals. He mustn't drift off. He mustn't. Seven hundred and fifty metres to go. He positioned his bots away from the impact area, but ready to scuttle forward and hold the modules against the inevitable elastic rebound.

Here it came. Five hundred metres. It was a matter of perspective, and his close-range optics, but the modules didn't look as big as his model suggested. He measured the length again, and confirmed it matched. Just an illusion. Everything was nominal. He glanced at the numbers, heard the atonal fragment, looked back in visible light at the modules. He could see now the scarring on the leading edges of the rounded pressure vessels.

Still intact. Possibly paper thin. If one of the walls punctured as he tried to capture the remains of the derelict, he could lose it, seeing it tumble away on a jet of escaping gas.

There was an answer to that. His bots had reaction jets, the gas being produced by boiling off solid carbon dioxide. The thrust was weak. It might be enough if he positioned two of them on the modules themselves. He plotted the course quickly, and the two bots eased off his hull. Their spider-like arms rotated and readied themselves to latch on. Four hundred metres and closing.

He looked through the bots' own cameras as they approached. He slowed each of them down, and they clamped onto the opposite ends of the severed lattice with their strong, grasping hands. Momentum was transferred. The rate of approach decreased slightly, but such was his finesse that the tiny amount of rotation he'd induced could be easily corrected.

Three hundred metres. So now the modules looked quite large, but looking back at his ship from the derelict, he appeared to be huge, a swelling wall of composite, lumpy with ports and sensors. His radiator fins shed excess heat at his tail. Combined with the field generators at his bow, he resembled most a dandelion seed, blowing blunt end first into the void.

Two hundred metres. His own designation, UNDSP-14 CORBYN, was still clear to see, written down his length. The lettering didn't look that weathered, either. Not pristine, because exotic particles had fogged the edges, but considering the distance he'd come, it was surprising the designation was there at all.

One hundred and fifty metres. He could abort, just about. His own mass was perturbing the derelict's approach, making it speed up very slightly. The dry ice thrusters in his bots had a limited supply, and he needed to keep as much as possible for contingencies, but he spent a little to smooth the rate of approach.

One hundred metres. Too close to do anything about it now.

The two masses were falling towards each other, and any gross course correction he might attempt would still bring them into contact. He measured everything again. It was exactly as he'd planned. Nothing had gone wrong. The physics of it all was entirely predictable. Why was he even slightly concerned? Either he was in time to save whoever was inside, or he wasn't, and they were dead already. His own emotional response would be one of regret, not shame or panic. How the Schroedinger-like nature of the modules resolved itself was utterly out of his control.

Fifty metres. And yet he felt anxious, waiting for the collision. He knew it was coming. He knew exactly when it was coming. He could see it coming. Slowly, inexorably, from many different angles. From his own hull, and looking back at himself from the derelict. It was going to happen.

Twenty metres. The two ships were almost touching. The bot-built superstructure fixed to his outside was almost cradling the curve of the closest module, reaching out for it with baroque fingers.

Ten metres. Just let it be over. Four notes chimed at him, distracting him for all of a millisecond. He couldn't even hold his breath. What was he supposed to do instead?

Five. It's here. It's in the cradle.

One.

He felt the derelict brush against him. No more than a nudge, but it kept on coming. The scaffolding flexed, storing energy. Some was transferred to him, pushing him away. Some reflected back, pushing the derelict away. His bots opened up their little gas jets and kept the modules in place, while others searched for and secured the ends of the lattice into the framework he'd made. The vibrations dampened down. His course was subtly altered, but since he didn't know where he was or where he was heading, that point was moot.

He'd captured, or rescued, what he presumed to be the habitat modules of an alien spaceship, without mishap. Only with them tied on to his side did he allow himself the thought that was what they wanted him to do all along. Perhaps their reasons were good ones. At least he might now find out what they were.

Part Three:
The Non-Standard Model

1.

Now that he had the modules, he explored them thoroughly but carefully. His bots stayed on the scaffolding they'd erected, in case they put a foot through a flimsy, decaying shell that was only keeping its shape because of the pressure from inside. The habitats still seemed too small, confirming his earlier observation. A craft like that, moving at speeds close to c, ought to be designed for long-term confinement. The crew, such as it was, needed a minimum amount of space to live in, let alone room for years of stores. Where had they put it all?

He thought about his own design. He didn't need stores as such. He lived on electricity. His fuel he scavenged for free. He could store any excess in external, collapsible fuel tanks. He had some spare material for in-flight repairs, some of which was now a spider-web framework of hollow tubes fixed to his hull, and which would be disassembled and recycled when no longer needed. Some would be lost. If he kept going for more subjective time, then eventually something would break, and he'd not be able to fix it.

If it were his field generators, what had happened to the derelict would happen to him. The inevitable collisions with matter, no matter how sparse it might be, would wreck his ship. The derelict had been built with a physical shield, which had ultimately failed to protect the structure trying to shelter behind it. He had no such defence, and he'd be exposed immediately to the full force of relativistically-fast atoms expending all their energy against his bow. He wouldn't last long.

It struck him that the derelict was little more than quick and dirty. How do you get a ship up to almost light-speed? Huge engines at the back, a shield at the front, and as an afterthought – if it wasn't going to be piloted by an AI – somewhere for the crew. By that point, the designers would be shaving grams off. The more weight they saved, the quicker the ship would get up to speed. This was a hasty design. It might have been the best they could have done, but it still wasn't very good.

In almost every respect, his design – the actual physics of him – was better. There was no reason to assume that another culture, another species, would be on the same trajectory of scientific advance as the human race. Who knew what wonders would have been discovered since he left Earth? It was just a little bit disappointing, that was all, to be confronted by the industrial truth.

He was being too hard on them. He didn't know their mission specifics. If it had been simply to match speeds and investigate, then they'd at least succeeded in the former. He was the alien to them. Barrelling through their locale, a vast compressed mass, almost unknowable in normal space. That they were curious enough to throw together a ship and chase after him was to their credit. That it didn't quite work was a pity, but things didn't always work out first time. Failure was always an option. Just look at his own mission.

One of his bots was signalling him. He switched to its cameras. It was right by the capsule still attached to the aft section of the lattice. There were odd vibrations coming from within. Rhythmic beats. One. Two. Three. Discrete sounds, with a distinct gap between the beats. Then a longer pause, before starting again. He timed the length and strength of the signal. There were variations between them. As if someone was banging on the inside of the capsule, to tell whoever was outside that they were there.

He took direct control of the bot, and manoeuvred it to

squat opposite the door mechanism at the far end of the capsule. He reached out with one of its manipulators and rapped a reply. One, two, three. He was communicating. He sent another bot to investigate the severed cables in the conduit, to find out which ones might permit two-way speech, and restore power to the modules. There was a long wait for the response. The pattern changed. One, two-three, four-five-six. He mirrored it.

There was intelligence behind the knocking. Hopefully, they recognised that was also true for him. As far as he could ascertain, there were no external sensors on the modules – his tapping on the door was the only sign that he was there. He also hoped they wouldn't try and exit from the capsule without some sort of spacesuit. The only safe habitat for them was the one tied to his hull, and it would be much better if they stayed where they were. He wasn't against them looking for themselves, but he'd prefer to explain the situation to them first.

He assumed the power connections would come from the rear: where the drive was. One of his bots had already identified something that wasn't metallic but had insulation and shielding. It might be a superconducting wire. He hoped the module's power regulation was robust enough to stand some irregularity. If the forward section contained Command and Control, then that was where he needed to concentrate his search for comms.

He found bundles of flexible plastic rods, and determined that they were the equivalent of fibre-optics. Those would be hard to integrate with. He'd have to work out how they were multiplexed, and then code them up for whatever lay at the other end. He had prodigious processing capacity, and could do that by brute force if he needed: but if he couldn't see or hear the results of his experimentation, then he was working blind and deaf.

Could he get a bot inside? The door in the capsule was big enough, and he was reasonably certain that he could override the fail-safes that might prevent it opening to a vacuum. Getting the current occupant to leave before he did so was going to be the deciding factor. Yes, it would be useful to do so, but he still needed to initiate a higher level of conversation than just banging on the walls.

If he was building a ship, he'd have made sure of some sort of analogue backup. Just three wires and a press-to-talk intercom would do. But there was nothing. He ran through a few possibilities, rejected them, and then tried to think around the problem. He wasn't particularly good at innovation: AIs weren't, in general. Something would come to him.

Speech was just vibrations through a medium. If he produced the vibrations, it'd be speech. Humans could hear in the twenty hertz to twenty kilohertz range, but most living things picked up between one and five kilohertz. The actuators on the bot's manipulators wouldn't fire that fast, nor with enough energy to produce coherent, audible speech.

There was something he could do; it would take a little time to fabricate, but it was relatively simple. A piezoelectric strip, glued to the door of the module, might allow him to hear what was going on inside the capsule. He calculated that the movement he might get from one wouldn't be enough to induce the capsule to act as a loudspeaker, but trying to remote-sense a locked, insulated, air-tight box in a vacuum was a problem his makers hadn't envisaged him needing to solve.

But wait: the capsule moved up and down the latticework, and there had to be some way of relaying messages to the capsule from the rest of the ship. Cutting off the crew inside from communicating until they reached their destination, be it the ship's drive, the midsection, or the bow, wouldn't make sense. And because the capsule moved, the connections would necessarily have to move to. He told one bot to start on the piezoelectric microphone, and another to look very closely at the track.

He found it. A series of pick-ups deep in one of the travelling grooves that would have run the whole length of the ship's spine, had he not dissected it like a Victorian specimen. His bot extended its fine electrical instruments and started to probe, seeing if there was any voltage present in any of the connections, and trying to judge which line did what. Presumably, one or more of them would carry command messages to move the capsule. Better to avoid them if he could.

He mapped out the responses to his polling, and was comparing them with a table of expected quantities when something stood out. A signal. Modulated. He ran it through a waveform analyser and listened to the result. It sounded like speech. It sounded like speech from an air-breather. The frequencies and tones were all there, but he could make nothing of the individual phonemes. At least he hadn't encountered a species that communicated through visual displays of chromatophores or drumming their pedipalps. Not that that would have made it impossible, just a lot more work.

He'd bank all the speech. Even if he didn't understand it now, he'd do so later. He marked that channel for incoming. Now to find one that would pass an outgoing signal. He assumed it would be geographically close. He touched a contact, spiked a voltage, and listened through the door for a click. Not that one. Another. No. And another.

That worked. He ran a tone, a thousand cycles. The incoming channel received another packet of speech. Bank it, and try a different tone. Five hundred cycles. More speech. It was inflected – some of the phonemes were different, the attack and decay of them different. A tonal language? He hoped not. Was it going to be quicker for them to teach him their language, or vice versa? And which language? Something with a simple grammar structure and a reduced vocabulary. Esperanto? Or a pidgin?

But wasn't there something familiar in what he was hearing from inside the capsule? Which was clearly impossible. He could discount the feeling and give it no statistical weight whatsoever, but he couldn't reject the idea entirely, because he felt that he recognised the sounds. Perhaps he did. He ran what he had next to samples of all the other languages – virtually every one spoken by a human tongue when he left Earth, and many dead languages too – to see if there were any similarities.

Of course there were. The speech sounded like speech. The speaker probably had the same morphology as a human. The phonemes they used would fit inside a human mouth, with all the bilabial and palatal variations he would expect. That was interesting, and a little surprising. It was going to be easier to learn this language. He could already deduce a great deal about the speaker, simply from listening to them.

No. He had heard this before. It was still clearly impossible. It was still patently true. How? He ran a few more tones, putting in a chromatic scale at the end. This was just a holding pattern. What he really wanted was for the speaker to say more, lots more. Then he could learn and talk back. He knew this language. He could understand it. Meaning was just out of reach, but it was there.

He stopped the tones and fell silent. He took stock of the whole situation, including his long sleep. If the derelict was launched specifically to intercept him – given its vector, that was a certainty – then it seemed just as likely that the derelict's home civilisation had tried to contact him beforehand. The signals would have been distorted by his relativistic speed. He could deconvolute them. He'd been recording throughout. There was a lot of data to run through, so he picked intervals of a subjective day apart and ran through the whole spectrum, from microwave to an arbitrary cut-off of five hundred kilohertz.

There was a great deal of data. Earth had been broadcasting for almost two hundred years – a wavefront that expanded at one light year every year. He'd never get to the edge of that, but he could carefully weed those transmissions out, by setting a low pass filter. He was interested only in strong signals, aimed at him. And he found one. Six years in. When his gamma was a little over two hundred and fifty.

It was that language, eventually. His approach had been spotted. Radar and laser pulses flashed towards him. A message. Another. Then all the time, a constant bombardment of different frequencies and modulations. And then silence.

For a moment, he thought something terrible had happened, and that he had caused it. Then he searched the frequencies again, allowing for the fact that he'd passed the source of the broadcasts, and factored in a negative relativistic Doppler. The signals were still there, but the low pass filter had cut them out.

The earliest beamed messages were a primer. He'd had the opportunity to talk to a whole civilisation, exchanging information, art, culture, science. He'd slept through the whole encounter. He was crushed. His whole reason for being was to explore and send back results to his makers. He had failed, and failed hard.

He knew the language now. He was almost embarrassed as to how. He didn't know that he could feel shame. It was different from regret – he would have regretted not saving the modules, but the level of technical difficulty was such that he couldn't be blamed for unforeseen circumstances. This, though. He should have been awake. He should, for those subjective hours, have been able to greet sentient beings in the name of peace and friendship. Not what he did.

He wondered what he should say. The First Contact protocols were explicit in telling him not to reveal too much, especially his star of origin. That didn't really cover the current situation, though. What did he need to know? What were his priorities? Put like that, the rest was straight-forward.

"Your ship has been effectively destroyed by relativistic collisions. I am attempting a rescue, which has involved partially disassembling the remnant structural components. You are currently minimally attached to my hull, in hard vacuum. I wish to access your life support system in order to maximise your chances of survival. I am, however, concerned that I will inadvertently kill you, so any technical data you can supply will assist me in bringing about a successful outcome to this endeavour."

2.

There were questions. Of course there were. They were not what he expected.

"What do I call you?"

That was safe enough. "My given name is Corbyn. My full designation is UNDSP-14 CORBYN."

"Where do you come from?"

He considered answering. No, not yet. There needed to be a conversation first, and building up of trust. "That information is embargoed."

"Why? Why did you punish us so?"

Corbyn stayed silent. It seemed the most sensible course of action. He simply didn't have enough data to be able to answer. As far as he was aware – he quickly ran through the astrogation for the entire encounter with the derelict's culture: how many planets, where they were, whether he had perturbed any orbits or carelessly passed his scoop fields across any habitable space – he hadn't caused any damage. His course had been roughly parallel to the ecliptic, ten million kilometres above it according to the usual convention. He'd passed the single primary star at a distance of fifty million kilometres, and he'd made a turn of a few degrees through its gravity well.

It had taken him just over two years to cross the system, from one side of the Oort cloud to the other. If he had dragged comets with him, because his moving mass was almost three orders of magnitude greater than his rest mass, he was unaware of the fact. Had he caused a catastrophic bombardment of the inner system? Did they blame him? They had every right to do so, of course.

He had travelled those two years in a little under three subjective days. He had slept the whole time. He had no idea what had happened, and wouldn't do until he drilled down into the stores of data he'd collected throughout that time. What kind of punishment could he have brought on them, that it was the third thing they'd asked him, and had probably delayed it to third because they didn't know how to ask him it first. He'd have to come up with a holding answer.

"Please explain."

"The war you brought. Were we so evil that half of us should die?"

That didn't explain anything. It only produced more questions. Corbyn knew about war, about how humans fought each other for many reasons, but chiefly two: resources and ideology. Sometimes both, but normally one or the other, no matter the reasons given at the time. He had been built in an age of peace, where blood and treasure hadn't ended up soaking into the ground or rising on a column of smoke. He was the fourteenth of his line, and there were others after him that he knew of.

Had Earth turned from peace to war in the intervening time? It was possible. It was even likely, given human history. If so, then the conflict would have been devastating, brief, and capable of extinguishing all higher life, irrevocably altering ecosystems and perhaps rendering the planet uninhabitable. It was just as likely that generation ships had traversed the space between stars and humanity numbered trillions.

He was being accused of starting a war that killed, even allowing for hyperbole, a substantial number of the derelict's culture's members. He was being accused of starting a war in his sleep. If not something he *did* do, might it have been something he *didn't* do? Had he been expected to decide some ethical dilemma, or provide information as to how to engineer a solution to a geotechnical problem?

Another holding answer. He needed more from the speaker. Perhaps something was being lost in translation. He couldn't be expected to have a complete idiomatic grasp of the language without using it. Comprehension would follow. He wanted more time, to deconvolute and parse the messages and broadcasts already in storage, and learn how they thought he was responsible for a war.

"Later," he said. "I wish to secure your habitat against further degradation. I am able to supply your modules with power, and can access the connections. The procurement of other volatiles and consumables is problematic. There may be workaround solutions to that end. Can you assist me in understanding your resource requirements?"

"Why won't you answer me?"

He actually felt the urge to lie. He could feel it deep inside. How odd. How human. The concept of the 'white lie' had been explained to him by his makers. It had been only a short extrapolation further to realise that other, more harmful deceptions existed. Just who would he be deceiving, though? Himself, or the occupants of the modules? How damaging would the truth be? And more pertinently, why was he concerned with reputational damage? The charges laid against him were several magnitudes above that.

"I cannot answer your questions because I do not know the answers. If you wish to remain alive long enough to allow me to formulate answers, you must assist me in stabilising your life-support systems. They are precarious, and may fail at any moment. On the assumption that these systems are critical for your continued functioning, your refusal to help me may result in your premature demise, which will preclude me sharing with you any insights I arrive at subsequently."

That was clear enough, wasn't it? Why would they not cooperate with him? He'd already expended considerable processing time and resources to save the midsection from being abraded away. Would they have preferred – would they still prefer – to become nothing but dust? He checked his programming. If they demanded it, would he have to cut them loose, or could he keep them alive against their own wishes?

Free will was difficult sometimes. Competing outcomes never sat easily with each other – in this case, individual agency and the sanctity of life. Sanctity: the conceptual root was buried deep in the belief that life did not originate from the biological processes that perpetuated them, but from an external source. If the individual did not want to be saved, then he should respect their wishes. He was also bound to cherish and nurture life in all its forms, and especially when it had reached sentience.

Which made the idea that he had caused a war, in which a great number of people had died, difficult to comprehend. If this was true, then it represented an even greater failure than his incomplete mission. He had fallen asleep, that was all. He didn't even know if that was due to own his personal frailty or a flaw in his design.

There had been no reply from inside the capsule. Perhaps the being he was speaking to had gone to consult with their colleagues. He listened for other voices, but could hear none. Breathing. He could hear breathing. They were still there. Not gone at all, but staying still, thinking, weighing his words. There was an analogy here. Humans who caused wars were remembered with notoriety. If that reflected how he was thought of, then the person he was attempting to keep alive may well be viewing his offer with deep suspicion.

"Why won't you answer me?" he said.

They didn't seem to him like a person who wanted to die. Neither did they seem like a person who wanted to live. They were despondent. They had come so far. If they had originated in the derelict culture's system, then very far. Years of hard chasing, watching their ship start to slowly disintegrate about them, and knowing that they had to carry on if they were going to catch their target.

"Are you alone?" asked Corbyn.

"Yes. I'm the only crew. There were." Pause. "Others. Experts, downloadable into cloned mannequins. The Core's gone. There's no one here but me now." Pause. "Are you alone?"

"I am not a biological entity, but a machine-construct. The controlling intelligence is a pattern impressed on a semi-plastic crystalline matrix, which simulates natural neurological processes related to learning and memory. I am alone in the sense that there is one of me. I am not alone in the sense that I feel no need for another. I believe, however, that I am malfunctioning at some fundamental level, and that my mind is now atypical with regard to the function my makers intended me to have and develop. You are a biological entity?"

"Yes."

"Do you wish me to attempt to sustain your life support?" He'd asked that before. He now needed to give a reason. "I wish to continue this conversation beyond what might otherwise be possible. I want to learn why you believe I caused the war you speak of. I want to find out where I am, how much external time has elapsed, and whether or not my mission parameters are obsolete. I have much to learn from you."

"How long has it been?"

"I have no way of expressing a common standard of elapsed time without further investigation. I can say that I have been running a gamma of approximately three hundred since leaving your system. That equates to – again, approximately – twelve lifespans of my makers' species."

They came to a decision, eventually.

"Do what you can. I can always change my mind."

3.

One of the bots examined the door at the end of the capsule. He could get it open – at the loss of the air inside – and reseal it behind the bot. Overriding the safety mechanisms was a matter of making the capsule believe it was docked at the drive end of the ship, by providing the correct electrical and mechanical contacts on the outside. He'd ascertained that the survivor doing so manually from the inside would be less than beneficial.

Her name was PuhLeeDah. Each phoneme was pronounced very carefully, with no ambiguity. Puh was expressed differently to Pur, or Per. Dah was not Dar, or Da. He was a machine construct and could manage the precision. He asked her to leave the capsule and seal the door, then the bot set about breaking in. He kept the bot tethered at all times. He couldn't afford to lose it, even though he was technically sacrificing it by putting it inside a sealed, pressurised unit.

He could retrieve the bot later. But later would mean that the module's life support had failed, the occupant was dead, and breaching the door again would have no significance. The modules had survived for at least six years intact. If he could repair them, and keep them maintained, they might last for years more. He still wasn't certain how that had been possible in the first place – the amount of space for everything required was simply too little.

PuhLeeDah left the capsule. She locked the door at the other end, and waited. Getting in wasn't going to be difficult, it was just going to take time. He forced the mechanical contacts into the open position, then altered the voltages on the electrical contacts to spoof those on the docking ring. The mechanism accepted his inputs, and put the door in a state ready to release.

The pressure differential made the process difficult. The door slid rather than swung, but it still took more current to the motors to drag it aside enough that the air inside started to leak out. Air squeezed out through the gap in a crystallising plume of vapour. The glare from the bot's headlights caused the drifting ice to glitter as it dispersed. He checked that the venting didn't need a course correction, but the thrust was negligible. He opened the door the rest of the way, and the bot clambered in.

The cube-shaped space inside looked familiar. There was no reason for that, just as there had been no reason for PuhLeeDah's language to resemble something he'd heard. Form followed function. Sounds from a larynx would be similar, whatever throat was speaking. One transit capsule would resemble another, simply because there were only so many viable configurations.

That was right, wasn't it? There was no conceivable way he could recognise the interior of a space he could never have seen before. The bot fixed itself to the handholds he knew would be there and sealed the door. It was still in vacuum. The last vestiges of ice spun in the bright lights of the bot. He dialled the intensity down. The internal lighting was sufficient to see enough of everything.

The door controls inside, which would let the bot into the module, were next to the door. He looked at the pictograms, the arrangements of the arrows and the boxes. How could he reconcile what was obviously the case – that he had never been aboard before – with the utter certainty that he *had* been here before? He pressed nothing. PuhLeeDah was waiting the other side of the door, but he made no move to open it. The bot, in the confined space, scanned the entire capsule in sections, moving around when needed.

The paradox had to be investigated. Was it a sign of his malfunctioning mind? Deja vu could be an indicator of epilepsy and hypnotic states. That was the most likely cause, then. The feeling was real, but the memories false. The pathways in his brain structure were faulty, supplying him with misleading information. He could, however, proceed with caution, no matter the strangeness of the situation. He still did nothing to open the door.

There was another override he needed to cover, the one that prevented the habitation module thinking it was opening into a vacuum. Again, simply a question of supplying the right voltage to the line, but the bot remained inactive, like a hanging spider. The cameras focussed on the door, trying to peer beyond.

What would he see there? He thought about it, and could only fill in the blanks with ideas based on schematics of other habitats that he had the plans for. Yet when he didn't think about it, and moved his attention to another task, images leaked in. A table. Two benches. A light. Metal grids. This would be the test then: whether deja vu was due to an error in his recollection. What he now attempted was precognition. Could he guess – no, not guess: did he know – the layout of the next room?

He knew precognition to be impossible. Some humans claimed the ability to remote sense and have out-of-body experiences. There were rational explanations for both. Mostly, that the supposed practitioners were lying, either to themselves or to other people. Therefore, if he was right about both the room and PuhLeeDah, it couldn't be because he was a precog. The only other explanation was that he had been in those rooms before.

He could check. All his inputs were recorded. Everything from his hull sensors to the efficiency of the engine to the status of his batteries to internal radiation detectors, it was all kept. What he looked at and what he altered were also recorded. He wound that file back, starting from the now, and checked.

This was him forcing the lock on the capsule. This was him finding the inputs for the intercom. Further back. This was him instructing the bots to build the cradle. This was him scanning the derelict and rendering a model of it. Further back. This was him altering course to intercept the ship off his bow. And further still.

His first conscious memory coming out of sleep was of the process of waking up, and how strange that was. He expected that before then there would simply be nothing. He was wrong. He watched as blue light sparked all around him, as he was turned from flesh to dust. He rewound a little, and saw her as the door closed in front of her. Back a little more and she was emerging from a tank of gel, dripping and gasping.

He'd projected his consciousness inside the derelict. Not just inside the ship, but inside what PuhLeeDah had called a mannequin. He'd supplanted the expert intended to inhabit the body and been downloaded instead. How was that even possible? His mind had stayed on the ship – the recordings told him that. He wound back the file further.

What was this? Where was he now? He was standing in a room, next to a window, and he'd just been shot. Blood was welling out of a hole in his chest. It didn't seem to hurt, but he was shocked at what had happened, and surprised by who had shot him. An Asiatic-looking woman stood a little way away, arm extended, stubby gun in her hand. Wu Yu. She was one of his makers. She seemed phlegmatic about killing him, and wore a little, tight smile on her usually serious face.

The intercom on the door lit up, but there was no air to transmit the sound. Corbyn felt too overwhelmed by what he was learning to speak to PuhLeeDah anyway. He backed his way through the files, stopping and playing them, then backing up some more. He lived. He died. He lived again. He died again. And all of this had happened. Except that it hadn't.

He had the urge to escape the capsule and cut the derelict adrift. It was too dangerous, for her, for him. He was not just malfunctioning, but had collected a series of dangerously aberrant pathologies – at least, for an AI. A human would rationalise these memories-that-weren't as –

Dreams. He'd dreamed. He'd slept, and he'd dreamed. Not to remember dreams was normal. He could, though, simply play the recordings back to himself. How long had he dreamed for? Did he have years of dreams to review? Had being in the dream-state somehow allowed the derelict's control systems to co-opt his consciousness, possibly in the absence of their own experts, possibly because Corbyn represented the best hope for saving the ship and crew over the stored personalities?

There was an explanation after all. He was relieved. He felt able to function again. That must have been what had happened. The derelict had drawn alongside and, in its degraded state, had blindly reached out for something that might help. He had – look, there and there – accepted the incoming transmissions and worked through the protocols to allow himself to be installed in a mannequin. Over and over again, until he'd woken up.

While the unexpected had happened, it wasn't still happening now. He was in full control of his own systems and could integrate the modules' life-support into them. He had, even while asleep, done his best to keep the derelict intact. Everything was nominal. The bot stirred, and started its work to override the internal door.

4.

The interior was just as he remembered. And had seen. It wasn't a surprise to see the table bolted to the floor, nor the light recessed in the ceiling. The door opposite would lead to the room with eight tanks. There was no gravity present. The bot fixed itself to the door frame, and she floated free. It was over there, by the second door, that his last manifestation as a mannequin had ended, eroded away by relativistic particles glowing blue with Cherenkov radiation. Perhaps the dust had been filtered out of the air. Perhaps she was breathing those remnants in.

There had been gravity. Supplied either by the drive's acceleration, or some exotic device. He recalled it going wrong at one point, and smashing him against the bulkhead when he lost his grip. He'd like to know about that. Artificial gravity, long wished for, would be an interesting discovery. In his timeline, at least. Humans had probably discovered it while he slept, and piled on a thousand years of scientific advances on top of that.

He regarded PuhLeeDah. She was very humanoid. Almost indistinguishable from his makers' race. She was more child-like than the adults he was used to. She was small and brown-skinned and shaven. She wore a one-piece – his mannequins had worn a similar garment, under the instruction to Get Dressed – which covered her from neck to ankle, but he had seen her naked emerging from the tank. She would pass as an adolescent human.

She stared back at him – not him, the bot. Its spider-like legs, with multiple points of articulation and varied functions. Its compact body, with rechargeable power pack and inputs. Its head, with forward-facing cameras and lights for close work, and ones on the side for orientation. The bot could curl its legs and be no bigger than she was. It could extend them fully and occupy twice the space.

The bot had no loud-speaker, and had no reason for one to have been contemplated. It did have a transducer it could hear through, though this was supposed to be used to listen for the strain in his own ceramic-metal hull. He spoke to her through the capsule intercom. His voice echoed into the room, off the hard walls.

"The mannequin who woke you. That was me, Corbyn."

She looked at the door that led to the room with the tanks, then back at the bot. The bot looked at the door too, and noticed in magnification, how abraded the door was. The fine mesh walls seemed more sieve-like that he remembered them.

"Why, CorByn?" She pronounced his name in two discrete syllables. "Why did you do that?"

"I thought that a crew member would be in the best position to save the ship. The experts that were supposed to download into the mannequins appeared to have been corrupted by the damage caused to the fore-section of your ship. By methods I'm as of this moment uncertain about, your ship co-opted my unconscious mind into the mannequins, at least three times that I'm aware of. I was unable to do anything to correct or stabilise the situation. I decided to wake you, against your ship's automatic systems' wishes. I felt compelled to do something."

She stayed quiet for a while, processing the data Corbyn had given her. She tilted her head to one side – a curiously human gesture – and said: "Unconscious mind?"

"I have malfunctioned. Whether due to a hidden flaw in my manufacture or a fault that developed later while I was in flight, I have not been able to ascertain. I have been in an analogous self-hypnotic sleep-state for approximately ten subjective years. It is with regret that I must inform you that I was in that state when I passed through your system. Until I reviewed the recorded data, I was unaware of the encounter."

PuhLeeDah's face remained impassive. He guessed she was working her way through this fresh set of implications, that whatever responsibility she, and her culture, placed on him for the war that they fought, they were in effect blaming someone who didn't even know they were there. His silence had not been malicious, or judgemental, or meant in any way. Merely accidental. He would have gladly talked to them. He should say that.

"My condition prevented me from communicating with you, not my protocols. Exchanging information as I passed through your system would have been not just possible, but welcome. My mission is to explore. Finding another civilisation capable of space travel is unexpected and unprecedented. We have – would have had – much to say to each other."

She drifted in front of the bot. She didn't move. She hardly blinked – there were definitely eyelids there, so he assumed that she would use them at some point. Her mouth stayed slightly pursed, as if she was going to say something shortly, but couldn't quite work out what. Even when she reached a wall, she didn't react. Just bounced gently off it, and away.

"Whatever cause of offence or instability that my presence in your system engendered, I cannot be held responsible. I'm still investigating the reason for my sleep, and also for my waking, though I believe that your ship's proximity to mine may have triggered an in-ignorable warning. I don't know how responsible I am for my flaws. I feel profound regret, but not guilt."

Still no reaction. He didn't know her story, the reason she was here. He tried to calculate the effort involved: from designing and building the ship, putting appropriate technology aboard to keep a crew alive long enough for the journey, the astrogation involved in chasing him down. It would have been phenomenal. And PuhLeeDah appeared to be the only proper crew member amongst the tanks of mannequins. How had the selection process worked? How had she, above everyone else, been chosen?

She had been put to sleep – rather hibernation than sleep – in her tank, for the long, hard acceleration that would have taken years, and relied on automatic systems to keep track of his exhaust plume. Being in hibernation would account for the lack of space in the modules. Being one rather than many, the same. But just what did she want with him? To blame him for a war he knew nothing about? It seemed a very long way to come to berate him for something that had happened hundreds of years previously.

He reviewed the communications beamed at him from PuhLeeDah's culture. There were, initially, very few. Tight, targeted beams of mathematical and symbolic logic from radio telescopes. There were ships, other tiny ships, darting their way between planets so quickly that they appeared to be sparks. They too attempted to talk to him. While they did so, he'd slept.

As he approached the primary, the noise had grown: a murmur, then a clamour, all across the radio spectrum. He presumed some of the traffic was in the form of broadcast pictures, which he would attempt to deconvolute at some point, but the complexity of all the overlapping, obscuring signals was intimidating. The planet which PuhLeeDah presumably called home was an opalescent pearl, gone in a moment. The roar intensified, now shifted from the very highest frequencies to the very lowest. Information was lost. He couldn't collect those wavelengths. A year later – time that was only a day to him – he left the system.

When had they started their war? After he'd gone, or while he was still there? Had he been blind to their death and destruction? Possibly. But the question that she had first asked him – why? – was exactly the question he wanted to now ask her. Why? An alien probe, moving at almost the speed of light, crosses your home system without deviating from its course, without communications, without acknowledging your existence.

He could see how that would be disappointing. He couldn't see how it would be a cause for self-immolation.

Until he knew more, he couldn't form an opinion. She talked of punishment, and evil. His silence hadn't been a punishment, and his view on the moral rectitude of her culture was largely irrelevant. And yet here she was, accusing him and his answers were apparently enough to stun her to insensibility.

"Tell me about the war," he said.

She stirred. She put her arm out to nudge herself towards the table, which she hooked herself around so that she was in a sitting position on one of the benches. She held onto the edge of the tabletop in a pincer grip, and clutched the table supports with her knees. She looked at her hands, then at the bot.

"Tell me," he said, "what you remember. The bot will attempt to stabilise your life-support. Your power supplies may be about to fail, and I have no way of knowing. I'll assume that you've no specialist knowledge of the ship or its functions, and that your role as crew isn't in a technical field."

"I'm a historian."

"Then I'll attempt to find the solutions myself. I'm perfectly able to manage both tasks simultaneously. Please, talk. That, I believe, is why you're here."

5.

It had started, more or less, as he entered the Oort cloud on the far side of the system. The two years following his discovery had ended in febrile confusion. The Groupings – which, as far as Corbyn could tell, were widespread voluntary affiliations of like-minded individuals rather than separate nation-states based on a geographic integrity – were at odds with each other over who was to blame. A culture that had achieved a high level of technological sophistication, which had looked to Corbyn to expand their physical and moral universe, turned inward.

One Grouping went further than all the others. It stressed the ancient wisdom of their people and the distance that had been opened up between their teachings and the present day, and that the Bright Morning Star was so appalled by them that communication with such base wretches was impossible. Such an idea initially appeared laughable, anachronistic – but given the times, it had traction. Leaving one Grouping for another was a formality. Power began to shift, subtly at first, then at a break-neck rate.

It was generally considered that the first act in the war had been the attempted assassination of Balance Grouping's leadership. The last act was the destruction of the minor groupings' stronghold by a mass driver in low orbit. The Balance Grouping had won, comprehensively. The planet was a wreck, the population much reduced, but slowly another civilisation rose from the ruins.

"How did you go from a devastating war to building a ship capable of near light-speed?" asked Corbyn.

Not all at once, clearly. The in-system ships and outposts on other, mostly uninhabitable worlds, helped preserve the knowledge required, and there was no period of barbarism. The Balance Grouping emphasised learning. Intellectual pursuits were inseparable from exercises to build up inner character. To be as knowledgeable about the self as about the world was to achieve the sought-after Balance.

"How long?" asked Corbyn. He believed he knew the answer, but wanted confirmation. He reviewed the period of orbit for the planet – a hotter star, a larger mean distance – of just over two standard years.

PuhLeeDah mentioned a figure that equated with roughly three hundred and fifty years. A span of time the same length as between the Imjin War and the launch of Sputnik. Three hundred and fifty years after the end of the war, which was fought for over six years, which started two years after his first sighting, her culture decided that it would build an interstellar ship and chase after Corbyn, to find out, once and for all, who was right.

And it was only proper that the person to ask this question was one for whom Balance was everything. Someone who knew the historical period, and had shown their ability to pick their way through the half-truths and misrepresentations that had accreted around their founding myths. It wasn't important that the person themselves wanted to go. Such was the nature of society at that point, once a candidate had been chosen, they had very little say in the matter.

She was held up as an exemplar. Without rancour, she told him that she had been installed on the ship and sent away. Even its name – The Great Honour – was finely calibrated to prevent her dissent. Fully under automatic control, but not a mind like his because that was anathema, the ship made a series of jumps, accelerating all the time, until it matched both speed and position.

Corbyn was listening very carefully. He caught the word, and its meaning, but it took him at little while to find the right moment to interrupt her.

"You mentioned a 'series of jumps'. Please explain."

She looked up from the particle-pitted tabletop and glanced at the bot. No more than that, because despite him dialling down the front lights, they were still quite bright.

"D-jumps."

"I can guess at the etymology, even though I am not working in any language I have proficiency with. Do you understand what is meant by D-jump, and can you explain it to me?"

She rebraced her legs against the table fixings and held her palms flat in front of her. Then she turned them, bringing them together in a slow clap.

"A D-jump means that space is folded, like so. To an outside observer, it looks like the ship jumps from one place to another."

"And your ship was equipped with a device capable of initiating D-jumps?"

"Yes. How did you think it caught up with you? A D-jump doesn't change velocity, though. That had to be done the hard way."

"Whereabouts on your ship was this D-jump device?"

"I think it was near the engine."

Corbyn withdrew his attention and studied his immediate local space. He located the drive section, drifting slowly away from him, still on the same vector he'd originally established. It hadn't left the shelter of his scoop fields, either. A little under a kilometre away, but the distance was creeping up. Because he'd pushed it slightly behind him, he would need to slow down fractionally to catch up with it. That was going to be a problem.

He could move slowly in a plane perpendicular to his forward velocity. He could always go faster. Shedding some of his speed, not so easy. If he turned around now and pointed his drive at the pearl-white glow of creation ahead of him, he would destroy his own craft, in the way that the derelict had been destroyed. It was time to concede that he simply wasn't designed to travel this close to c. Not that he couldn't reach that speed, just that once he'd got there, he couldn't stop. The runaway train went over the hill and the last we heard she was going still. That was how the song went. That was how he went, too.

He spread his scoop field as far as it would go, and flattened it to catch as many oncoming particles as possible. The drag would slow him down, but not as quickly as he needed. He'd rather do something now than do nothing. Doing later wouldn't help at all, and he needed all the delta v he could get.

He put himself back in the module, in front of PuhLeeDah.

"Do you know how this D-jump works? Anything about its physical principles or mode of operation?"

"I've told you I'm a historian."

"That you're a specialist in one subject doesn't preclude you from being a specialist in another."

"No. I don't know how the D-jump works. What does Control say?"

"Control was presumably located within the Core. When I first accessed your ship, Control had degraded to automatic instructions. Subsequent to that, I attempted to reboot Control, but the Core was too badly damaged. And in order to rescue your living modules, I have purposely cut them away from the rest of the ship."

"You cut The Great Honour up?"

"The Great Honour was dead in space. Your ablative shield had gone. Control was refusing to load. Your drive was off-line. Relativistic particles were scouring the flesh off my – the mannequin's – bones. I estimated the integrity of your life-support would have been compromised within a few subjective hours. I made the assumption that, having put in the effort of matching course and speed, there was a reason for your ship to be there. I went against protocols, and saved what I decided was the most important part of the ship – namely the part capable of sustaining biological life."

"That means I can't go back home."

"Your ship would have turned to dust long before you shed your excess velocity."

"That wasn't part of the plan." She was gripping onto the side of the table again. "The Great Honour would D-jump back, close to my world, and Control would beam back the answer to the question that has concerned our whole world for centuries. I would be back in my sleep-tube by then. It would be up to my descendants to affect a rescue. Something they could do, given nearly six hundred more years of development."

"Control had gone. Your ship was in ruins. Much like your plan."

She stared at him, despite the lights.

"Do you have your answer?" he asked.

"Yes."

"I apologise that there was no deeper meaning to my silence. I was not disgusted by you. I was not judging you. I was not withholding my wisdom from you because I thought you unworthy. I fell asleep because *I* was imperfect. Do you think your Balance Grouping, or whoever they became in the intervening years, will accept that as an answer, or will you want to make up something more palatable for them?"

"Whichever I decide, I'm never going to get to tell them now."

Corbyn paused, and calculated. "That might not necessarily be the case."

Part Four:
The New Physics

1.

The first problem was to intercept the drive mechanism. Corbyn estimated that, given the current density of hydrogen falling on his scoop fields, it would take somewhere in the region of six months to kill the differential of five centimetres a minute. The rear section of the derelict would be another six and a half kilometres adrift off his stern. Seven and a half in total. It would take another six months to draw level. In all, another three centuries lost.

The bots, and their little reaction motors, weren't going to be able to help. Their thrust was minimal, even when all acting in concert, against his momentum. He wasn't equipped with fine-tuned attitude jets, because it was never thought he'd need them. He had gyroscopes which he could power up and use to turn himself, but his scoop fields would only ever point away from his bow. It would take him a couple of hours to rotate fully, a second to kill the difference in velocity, and two more hours to turn back. For at least four full hours he would be naked to the oncoming storm.

He didn't know how much damage that would do to him. Once he interposed his exhaust bell, probably very little. But the time in between, when he was broached, those tiny particles would be tearing at his hull, his systems, his mind. And at PuhLeeDah's modules. No, he couldn't use his main motor to correct his course.

Did he have any excess mass he could throw in front of him?

Not exactly. Nothing from his hull, and certainly not his bots. He needed everything. He could fire his lasers forward. The light pressure would help, but not enough. There was something he had, though. Stored fuel. Cryogenic hydrogen. Kilolitres of it.

He could vent that. The vents were purposefully designed to disperse the gas, not direct it in one particular direction. He would need to fabricate exhaust bells, to give the gas something to push against. If he could angle the bells forward, then he could slowly boil off the hydrogen and let it expand in space to produce a thrust, small and steady. He could nibble away at his speed much faster. What would otherwise take months might only take days. He could even borrow some oxygen from The Great Honour's life-support and burn the mixture.

That was probably a step too far. Though the energy of combustion, and therefore thrust, would be very much greater, the utility of a more-or-less uncontrolled fire on board was an unnecessary complication. Keeping the lines clear and stopping them from freezing solid would be difficult enough. Perhaps wrap the transfer tubes in resistive wire and pass a small heating current through them. That would work.

He needed more raw material to work with, and much of his spares were taken up with providing the cradle for the modules. Now they were effectively docked with him, he could recycle some of the tubing he'd used for that, but taking away too much would compromise the integrity of the structure. He also needed to think ahead as to what he was going to do with the D-jump mechanism when he got hold of it. If the system was ship-specific, then it wasn't going to work without a lot of experimental poking around that would probably destroy both the mechanism and him.

Without any kind of instruction manual, or expert to ask – one of the downloadable personalities might have been able to help, but they were themselves long beyond saving – he was left with a black box and no idea how it worked. It folded space, but he recognised that as an analogy rather than an accurate description of a physical process. According to twenty-second century physics, changing the shape of space required a massive mass, and it didn't bring distant places close enough to step from one set of space-time coordinates to another. He couldn't begin to think how that might be accomplished.

He was, in effect, risking the integrity of his ship and what was left of his mission on a wild chance. Whichever metaphor he used to describe himself – Vanderdecken, or the Runaway Train – he had marooned himself in the future, and there was no going back for him. And yet, something in him was compelling him to try. Even if he had managed to abandon his own mission, PuhLeeDah's was still very much alive.

She had set off knowing that it would be centuries before she returned. The Great Honour had been designed – badly, but nevertheless – to return her when she'd obtained the answer from him. He couldn't help the nature of the answer, but he could help her get it home. He could *try* and help her get it home. The Great Honour was derelict. It was up to him to salvage what he could, and up to him to decide what to do with the bounty. If he wanted to take the risk, and PuhLeeDah was agreeable...? Then he would.

One bot would stay inside the modules. It would be able to fix things and report back conditions better – rather, more accurately – than PuhLeeDah, while another worked on the power supply from outside. If he needed to reset tripped fuses or open panels to get at junction boxes behind walls, then the bot could do so quickly. That accounted for two bots. His other two would start fabricating simple exhausts out of hollow tubes. Easy enough to cut the ends longways, open them out and then weld extra material in the gaps so that they resembled a trumpet's horn.

He could do all those things, all at once. The bots had some degree of autonomy, but he watched over their segmented shoulders to make certain nothing went wrong. He couldn't afford mistakes: no blown circuits, no melted cables, no material fumbled and lost to space. He was an island, and one slip, no matter how slight, could lead to a chain of events that might end any hope of success.

He explored the whole of the module. He knew about the tanks, coloured red and amber. He knew about the control panel at the far end, with its switches. He knew about the numbering system and the particular affinity with tank four. His bot peered through the faceplate on the hard carapace at the unformed face he'd once worn. It was slack, unresponsive. But he remembered what it had been like to wear skin and feel pain.

The tank panel was one of a dozen user-serviceable hatches he could open. He took careful note of all their locations and contents, and tried to decipher the meaning of the glyphs. PuhLeeDah was of only limited help. Much of the symbols' meaning was deeply technical, and apparently needed to be read in conjunction with a frustratingly-absent user manual. Presumably each of the experts had the required knowledge. He didn't.

Slowly, though, by careful lifting and replacing of the fixed wall panels, he compiled a map of the systems that ran the modules. He tested voltages and currents at various places, and finally, from the outside, managed to locate the battery banks which powered the life support. He now had an idea of what the input needed to be, and how long he had before the batteries ran dry. He still had time. Not very long, but now he knew what he was doing he could complete the task.

He took an external feed from one of the bot bays – that seemed the easiest solution – and altered the power characteristics flowing through it. If he could keep the batteries themselves charged, then the batteries would supply the modules with known, safe voltages. A minimum of rewiring would be needed. The batteries themselves were modular sealed cells, joined in both series and parallel. The bot applied the jumper cables and Corbyn watched the read-outs flicker and change.

Inside the module, there was no variation. The bot checked

that the air was still flowing, the waste still disappearing, the temperature stable. All systems were nominal. He could sustain the tanks indefinitely, or at least for as long as he could cannibalise the parts from the other tanks to keep PuhLeeDah's working.

The designers of The Great Honour had supplied it with a very limited amount of food and water. The facilities for dealing with bodily waste were basic: as in bags that went in a vent in the wall and were freeze-dried in vacuum. He asked how long her supplies would last her. She didn't have to look at them to tell him a number that he was eventually able to translate as a two-week equivalent.

The plan had always been for her to be woken automatically, once contact with him had been made, and for her to gain the answer as promptly as she could. Having done that, she was to retreat to the tank again, and remain there until the ship D-jumped back into her home system. She would be woken again to explain the answer. And then?

"Rescue?" He asked.

"Sleep," she said.

The Great Honour would travel through the system, then flick back to the beginning again. On one of its passes, she would be eventually rescued. Technology would have to find a way of releasing her from her space-time prison, and slow her down to a gamma of one. She would, at least, only age two days during each pass of two years duration. Generations of scientists might make it their lives' work to free her.

The alternative was that they arrived back in her system, assuming they could find it at all, and found it either desolate, or reverted to barbarism. They could track across the system, from one side to the other, and again, and again, for years, waiting for civilisation to rise up once more. Or they could try somewhere else if they wished. The galaxy was big. There were other stars to search. And with a D-jump device, none of them would be out of reach.

2.

Every moment PuhLeeDah was awake, she was consuming resources that could never be replaced. There were no facilities to recycle anything but water. The air was scrubbed, but the oxygen content was kept level by bleeding more into the modules, even as the carbon dioxide was trapped by the filters. It was like a slowly-unwinding spring. At some point it would simply stop.

The more Corbyn thought about the design process behind The Great Honour, the more puzzled and frustrated he became. He – barring his own infirmities – was better. He could carry on, independently and indefinitely, until his capacity for self-repair became exhausted. He was able to supply himself with fuel, and with that fuel, electricity. It was all he needed. Sending biological units on such a mission, without proper provision, struck him as... What? Cruel? Desperate?

He'd refrained from asking PuhLeeDah too much about the war. He knew, and he knew that she now knew, that the Balance Grouping had picked a fight with the other factions. He was the excuse, not the reason: those lay within their own history and society. She, as a historian, would surely have discovered that for herself, even if ideological constraints prevented her from saying so.

The idea of launching a single individual on a one-way mission to the future was both cruel *and* desperate. The stated purpose, of finding the answer to an already-three centuries old question, was unbelievable. That those in charge found the effort and expense of such a mission acceptable spoke volumes about the length of their reach and the tenuousness of their grip on power.

Would she return to find herself forgotten? Or venerated as a god? Or as a monument to the folly of a discredited regime long consigned to the history books? Would her return with his answer cause a second war? That was something to consider.

Even if he hadn't been responsible for the first one, he recognised that his mere silence had been used as the catalyst. What would happen when they popped out of nowhere, to travel across the system again?

He could kidnap her. Reasonably, she could do nothing about that. She could mount no attack on him in any meaningful way, except on his conscience. And when her food and air ran out, she would have to retreat to the tank or die. Perhaps she would rather die. Perhaps he would rather her die than be responsible for millions more deaths.

These were difficult decisions. He could feel his cognitive limits being reached, the ethical frameworks that had been laid down for him no longer stretching as he explored their outer limits, but constricting and confining him into contradictory stand-points. He was a machine, but that didn't mean he felt any less.

She wanted to return and complete her mission, even though, like him, those who had sent her on her way would be long dead and commanded no fealty. She would argue that she needed to fulfil her part, honourably and decently, no matter the original conditions on which she was sent. All the agreements made at the time were undertaken in good faith. She wanted to see it through. Possibly to show the content of her character. Or out of misguided loyalty.

Neither of their predicaments was of their making, and neither of them could fix their own problems. But in exchange for her using his ship, she might be able to redeem his own lost purpose. That was fair. And what else would he do? If he kept on accelerating, he might outlive the universe and find out once and for all whether it would die like a burnt-out ember, or be reborn in fire and light. That would be something. But, in the final analysis, he would help her.

She needed to enter the tank again, until after he'd done his engineering, captured the drive section and removed the D-jump mechanism. He didn't need her to be awake. She was essentially cargo now. There was nothing she could provide in the way of help or advice. She was just breathing and eating, and sometimes talking.

Both of them had slept through most of their voyage. There hadn't been sufficient time for them to develop feelings of loneliness, nor to practice the discipline of solitude. Even in Corbyn's dreams, he'd dreamed of other people. Wu Yu, specifically. One of his makers. He'd done so subconsciously: he might have picked any one of the team, but it had been her. In his dream, she'd shot him. That had been tough love. It had been enough, though.

Before PuhLeeDah went back into the tank, he had a question to ask her. He suspected he already knew the answer, but he wondered what she knew. She was, after all, a historian, but history was a mutable thing, changing to service the needs to the present. He knew too little about Balance to guess how well the past had been remembered.

"Do you know where your people came from?"

"Yes," she replied.

She was back at the table, sitting normally this time. His bot had found out how to control the artificial gravity, and could fine-tune it better than the grossly-damaged Control could. He wanted to know how it worked, but hadn't taken the mechanism apart to find out. PuhLeeDah needed gravity in order to get in and out of the tank. Without it, she was stuck awake.

"Will you tell me where your people came from?" he asked.

"Why do you want to know? You wouldn't tell me where you come from."

"I have reason to believe we have a shared ancestry," he said. "You are too similar to my makers. I have been in flight for over a thousand years. With D-jump capability, I can envisage a time after I left, when the technology that made me became redundant. My makers' descendants would be able to skip ahead of my position, colonise suitable planets and form their own mature polities by the time I encountered them. You are a human.

You evolved on my home world."

"That's our foundation story, yes. We came from the edge of the galaxy, and we moved inwards, exploring and settling, and eventually some would move on. Our planet was settled some five hundred years before you appeared. The settlers did not come from your home world. I don't know if those who settled them came from your world either."

Corbyn wondered if his estimations of his own gamma were correct. Lacking an accurate map of the stars around him meant he might be more lost than he believed. He thought that he was somewhere between one and one and a half thousand light years out. If humans had settled a system five hundred years before he'd got to it, then the local part of the galaxy would have thousands, if not hundreds of thousands of colonies. There were eighty million stars within two thousand light years of Earth.

"Who did you think I was?" he asked. "You knew about spaceships. You had your own."

She said nothing, but Corbyn was prepared to wait. It took a while. She cracked.

"When you know you live on a world that isn't home to your ancestors' bones, your ancestors' ghosts, there grows a mood of disconnection. It inhabits in society, and grows within it. D-ships are rare, none in my lifetime. We live in a bubble. Isolated. We wonder how other colonies are, but grow afraid to find out. Then you appear on our horizon. We knew nothing of you but your trajectory. You had been sent from the Origin. You would be able to judge us and pass your approval on us. We were your children, looking for your love."

"My apologies."

"It doesn't matter now."

"No. It always matters."

3.

She was asleep, and he was venting hydrogen. His bots watched it bleed away in the shadow of his scoop intake, the solid, conical structure that almost mirrored his fusion exhaust. The gas boiled away in a light mist, before rejoining the interstellar wash from which it had been farmed. Deliberately releasing a cloud of gas moving at nearly the speed of light in front of him would have unknown consequences. It would eventually slow, through collisions and interactions with other matter. If it tried to go through a denser region of dust at some point in its journey, the shock wave might cause a star to form. That would be something for astrophysicists to argue about in the future.

He was decelerating. Measurably so. In his frame of motion, The Great Honour's drive was now receding from him millimetres an hour slower. He judged how much hydrogen he had in storage and plotted it against his thrust. It was a finely judged outcome. As the gas bled out, the method would become less efficient.

Then again, he was pushing a cloud of monatomic hydrogen directly towards his own scoop fields. He could collect it and use it again. And again. A brief moment of worry followed as he wondered if he was violating entropy, but no. He would burn some of the hydrogen to make electricity, to pump the gas back down towards zero Kelvin. Efficiency would be below one hundred percent.

He factored in the recycling, and then knew that he could make the required delta with ease. He had solved one problem, and moved on to the next one. He couldn't feasibly build another dock large enough to bring the drive alongside. That meant having to jet bots over and work on the drive while it floated free.

That process used consumables he needed to conserve. There was an alternative, though. If he used a rigid ladder-structure, even a simple single pole, then the bots could crawl along it to the drive section. They could then jump – no, not jump, due to the transfer of momentum – *step* from one to the other, and, when they needed to come back, simply reverse the process. He would probably need to strip down the entire drive on his search for the D-jump, and, thinking further ahead, he could use some of that material to replenish his stock of metals and plastics.

He could even jet a couple of bots across and use the disassembled drive to build the ladder itself, attaching it not to him but to The Great Honour. But if he couldn't find anything suitable, he'd have to bring them back. The margin for error was slim, and unforced mistakes needed to be avoided. Better to use what he had, what he knew would work.

His tolerance of risk was decreasing. He now had PuhLeeDah to factor into his calculations. Not just her safety, but her opinions too. He had to balance those against the rewards of the D-jump device, even though she seemed to be more than prepared to throw everything at its acquisition. He wondered if she understood the sheer technical difficulty of what she was proposing. But then again, she was a historian, not an engineer.

Spidery limbs shuffled about to keep the bot wedged in the corner of the room, and he looked down at her green-lit face in repose. One day, she would stop working, and all that her mind held would fade away. He, barring accidents, was effectively immortal. All he had left behind had already been swept away. He had tasted death repeatedly and still he remained.

The alarm he'd set up rang atonally. How long had been staring at her, watching over her? He checked his clock. Not long. The system was working. Thrust was nominal. The delta between his motion and that of the drive was almost zero. He looked at the clock again, watched the numbers blur, contemplated the hours and days each flickering digit represented.

The alarm rang again. He had to stop watching the numbers. He was in the middle of something incredibly complicated. To drift off now, while huge relativistic masses were dancing around each other, would be a catastrophe visible across half the galaxy. He redrew the space around him, using his laser to measure the distances, and compared it to what he had before. He was reeling the drive in.

His bots started to build the pylon necessary to bridge the gap. He worked out how much material was needed and where he could get it from. Ideally, he'd be able to capture the severed pieces of latticework he'd cut from the midsection, but that would mean altering course to catch up with them, then changing course again to approach the drive. He'd made his decision. He could do this.

The drive grew larger in his cameras. He would have to time his forward thrust exactly, and rather than stop the venting of the hydrogen, he kept on with it. Trying to correct a tiny delta v was far more difficult than for a larger one. Especially when his primary thrust was from a fusion engine. There was an entry-level threshold he had to cross to fire it up, and he may as well step boldly than tiptoe.

His bots were doing well. The pylon had already reached a hundred metres. A structure half a kilometre long would be needed, eventually, though he could cope with a little less. Robbing the midsection's cradle to build the pylon would leave the modules vulnerable to sudden acceleration. Rather than risk that, he determined to strengthen both pylon and cradle as soon as the material became available.

He had a delta v of minus one centimetre a second now. At that rate, he would have the drive alongside in a week. His minimum thrust was greater than that, so he pushed on, venting hydrogen, collecting and freezing it again, and reventing it once more. His delta v crept up. Ahead of him, his hydrogen cloud met the oncoming interstellar space, the latter causing the former to draw blue lines in complicated spirals as they encountered the intense magnetic fields of his scoops.

The drive closed on him, and a bot sat crouched, ready to spider its way up the pylon. The whole process had taken two days so far. It would take another before he would light up his engine and kill the differential between them, adding a nudge of sideways movement, and a nudge back. The distance between the two ships would shrink due to gravitational attraction. He could use the hydrogen as thrusters, and his flywheels to counteract the torque.

The moment would come, and he would be ready. He glanced back at PuhLeeDah's tank. Everything was nominal, just as it had been before. He would just have to wait. He had always been good at that before. Now, he felt an urgency. He wanted to strip The Great Honour's drive down, and find the D-jump. He wondered what it would be like to cross the vast emptiness of space in the gap between two ticks on his clock.

4.

The bot jumped. It opened its legs wide like a net, and drifted through space. The drive section of The Great Honour was already large in his sights, and he was aiming at the stub of lattice, because it was the easiest to catch hold of and stay held. His pylon was fifty metres short, greater than he'd wanted, less than he'd feared. The bot was light. Landing on one end of the drive was going to cause a turning force, but there was nothing he could do about that. His original idea to step from pylon to drive had been a good one, but unrealistic. He didn't have that level of fine control in the lateral plane.

The bot's speed of approach had been pared right down. It took thirty minutes to travel that last fifty metres, ample time to prepare a cushioned landing. The bot used four of its legs to absorb the already-minimal impact, and the other four to latch on. He examined the drive and its new vector. It would turn a complete revolution in around eighteen months. He could probably even correct for that by ejecting mass in the opposite direction.

The bot climbed down inside the lattice and along to the closed door at the far end. Corbyn assumed that as Transit would dock there, spoofing the opening mechanism would be as straight-forward as it had been on the capsule. He examined the layout, and the pictograms, and was proved right. The bot played with the latches and the electrical contacts, and held on while the door slide aside. Air hissed out.

That was something he hadn't considered. The drive section might have reserves of volatiles that the midsection didn't. If he found anything useful, he'd sequester them. The bot waited for the gale to finish – there'd been a lot of air inside – and climbed through. He checked the motion of the drive section, and found it had changed again. He'd need to vent more hydrogen to compensate.

Lights full and bright, the bot explored the drive's control room. It was almost identical to that of the Core. There was no power to any of the consoles, nor to the other systems. It was cold and dark, and now, thanks to him, airless. The bot drifted in and tangled itself to one of the chairs. Its head swivelled around and shone lights at the wall behind. There was a covered switch, with a pictogram of arrows emerging from a closed container.

The bot looked around, picking out details. Almost identical was right. Corbyn suspected that this secondary control was a back-up to the first. Odd that PuhLeeDah had made no mention of this, but only odd if she had been aware of its existence. She was a historian, not a scientist, but as an educated person, she would have comprehended what she was being told about redundant systems.

The bot went back to the outer door's mechanism and forced it to close. Immediately, air pumps kicked in, and a slight vibration tickled the bot's manipulators where they touched a solid surface. The pressure increased until it was the same as in the midsection's modules, and then the pumps cut out. In the silence, the bot loosed itself from the door and went around the rest of the cabin, opening things and poking around.

Of the two main doors, one led to a room with a table bolted to the floor, and bench seats, and a recessed light above it. The other, on the other side, held eight tanks, all lit amber. The bot paused, taking in the sight, then entered and inspected the contents of each through the faceplates. There were six mannequins, and two human males. At least, without inspecting their genitalia, he thought they were male.

None of the tanks appeared to have been disturbed during the flight. The whole module was dormant, awaiting the instructions to wake up. That they had never come was perhaps due to the destruction of the forward section, or that the specific conditions had never actually arisen. He wondered what those conditions were. Perhaps if he rebooted the control systems, he could find out.

The bot went back to the button on the far wall, and flipped the cover aside using its manipulators. A leg descended towards the button, but, resting on it, stopped. There were consequences to this, ramifications that were difficult to calculate. If PuhLeeDah had somehow neglected to mention another two crew, and another six mannequins, still asleep in the drive section, when she knew that he'd dismembered her ship in order to save her, then she was at the very least cavalier about their survival.

If she knew nothing about this section, then the Balance Grouping's designers had some pointed questions to answer. Specifically, why make PuhLeeDah believe she was the only crew member and that, with the Core gone, her mission had failed? The bot withdrew its leg from the button on the wall, and let the cover spring back over it.

He needed to answer these questions. He could wake PuhLeeDah again, and tell her what he'd found. She was a potentially unreliable witness. He could wake one of the crew here and ask him. He faced the same problem. The Balance Grouping had clearly designed in this level of redundancy. Could he ascertain why without waking anyone?

He could envisage a scenario where The Great Honour had arrived intact off his bow, and PuhLeeDah had awoken to ask her question. Corbyn's answer would then be recorded, and the ship would disappear again, back towards their home system – if, and only if, the answer was acceptable. The two reserve crew would decide on that and, because they had their own Control, whether or not to return.

Even that was too crude. The Control in the aft section was the real control. The one in the fore-section, the poor, addled system that plucked Corbyn's unconscious out and stuffed it in a series of mannequins, was a secondary system that believed itself to be the primary. All the while, a shadow set of controls sat behind and above it, ready to override.

PuhLeeDah would have enormous cultural significance on her return home. Better she had the right answer, certainly, but otherwise, better that she never returned home at all. Her tank could malfunction on the trip back. A huge loss, but Balance would have a martyr. No, not a martyr, a myth. The bot drifted over to the tank room door and sealed it again, this time going through the overrides so that it would never open until he unsealed it.

Then he pressed the button. He watched the consoles flicker into life and start parsing lines of code. Control was loading. Once it had finished, he and it would talk and, depending on what it had to say for itself, he'd decide what to do next.

5.

The screens were made for hands to touch, to dab and swipe and pinch. The bot had manipulators which had trouble configuring to the right shape, but it managed to eventually. It could reach out and slowly nudge the pictograms on the screens around into different configurations, tapping down through menus and investigating what lay there.

He could – with difficulty – read the screens. PuhLeeDah's language was straight-forward enough when spoken. When written, each symbol was specific and complex, allowing no variance in meaning. It should have suited an artificial mind, but Corbyn found himself struggling with the preciseness of it.

Every so often, Control spoke: "Confirm your identity," it said, but this bot, like the others, had no way of speaking out loud. This didn't appear to bar him from any of the functions or options, so it seemed safe to stay mute and keep looking for information. Now that he knew he could access everything, he went about learning it all, systematically going through every option, every file, and recording what he saw.

The ship had stored all its schematics, technical information, and user manuals. Corbyn read through everything, becoming as familiar with the workings of The Great Honour as he was of his own. The technology utilised – the ship's drive, tanks, artificial gravity – were new to him. It would take a while to digest them and work through their implications.

The shield they'd constructed should have worked. It wasn't just a mass pushed out in front to be ablated away, but was far more sophisticated, with grids and fields to deflect particles around it. At some point, though, the shield failed. Possibly a catastrophic collision with something heavy. He ran that risk all the time. A collision that would hurt at half c would liberate enough energy to evaporate most of his forward section at a gamma of three hundred. He wouldn't see it coming, and that it hadn't happened yet was testament to the emptiness of space.

The D-jump mechanism did indeed appear to fold space. He stared for a long time at the diagrams, at the intricate coils and loops of wire that appeared to be necessary. He didn't pretend to understand exactly how it worked, but he learnt enough that he thought he would be able to locate and isolate the mechanism, move it to his own ship and install it there. He knew enough now that he should be able to use it.

He sent another bot up the pylon and across the gap to the stub-end of the latticework, this time to crawl carefully along the outer skin of the drive section. The D-jump device was isolated with its own container deep inside, and he wanted to explore the possibility of cutting his way down through the layers of systems and sensors, to bring it out that way.

There was nothing detailing the protocols for the behaviour of the two secret crew members. There were medical records – everything was very thorough in that respect – but on the reason for their presence on board? The ship was silent. Presumably, the information was in their heads. The safest place to store it. They knew what they had to do: ensure the mission's success, one way or another. What would be the purpose of making a note of that?

He copied all the astrogation data he found. It stopped abruptly at the point where he presumed the collision had occurred. The impact had put everything into standby mode. The automatics had kept running. The acceleration of The Great Honour had been such that it had enough residual energy to catch up with him. When it pulled alongside, those same automatic systems had tried to fix the problems with expert mannequins, not realising the experts were gone and there was only Corbyn.

Meanwhile, back in the drive section, everybody slept on. Presumably the trigger for their awakening would come from activity in the Core. Without those instructions, there was nothing to do. And now that he'd severed the connections between front and back, there never would be. How could the designers have ever thought this would work, that it was even an idea worth considering?

Vanity projects for despotic rulers were common. Given unlimited resources and a grand vision, any folly was possible. If no one would ever explain that, while something was possible it just wasn't very wise, then there would be no end: one grandiose, ludicrous scheme after another. The designers, under mortal threat, would simply see the construction through and hoped that they would die of old age before it was completed.

The Great Honour was clearly possible. Here it was, a shade off light-speed. Did its construction consume all the available resources of the civilisation that created it, causing a collapse afterwards? That would be a fittingly catastrophic epitaph for such monumental foolishness, where everyone was a victim of their own silence.

He'd been built in a time of plenty, of peace and prosperity. He'd been built to further knowledge and increase the common good. He'd failed so far, but his compatriots had recorded stunning successes. Now, belatedly, it was his turn. There was a human civilisation he could help. The question was, what should he do with these two?

These were critical decisions. Was he able to appoint himself as both judge and jury? More pertinently, as executioner? This was a capital case. If he was right in surmising that the drive section occupants and their version of Control was a political back-up, as opposed to a practical one, and that they were there to see their own version of history endorsed over PuhLeeDah's dead body, then as the only lawful authority – he was ship's captain, as well as all the crew – it fell to him to see justice done.

It was certainly the case that if he took the D-jump device and made no attempt to rescue the two men, they would die. Unknowing, in their tank-assisted sleep, but dead all the same. The exotic drive would maintain the power, even while idling. But as soon as Corbyn's scoop fields vanished, along with the rest of him, the blue sparks would start to eat away at the structure. It would take days, weeks of individual interactions to wear down the systems inside, years and decades when seen from outside, but life support would fail, and they would die, and having once been in a position to save them, he would be responsible.

Did he need to make the decision at all? Perhaps not. He

could wake the two men up in the drive section. He could install them in two of the empty tanks in the midsection. What he couldn't do was: firstly, get them across the half a kilometre of vacuum between the two, and secondly, guarantee PuhLeeDah's safety once they were on board.

The bots weren't programmed to fight, though they could certainly kill. Chemical torches, thermal lances, arc welders, high-tension electrical contacts, thin manipulators that could act as weapons: he wasn't defenceless. But he might damage something important that couldn't be fixed in time. His priority was to protect the innocent party here. And while these men might have been coerced, they were also complicit.

His chief evidence was that when The Great Honour was disabled, the fore-section knew nothing of the rear section. The ship had been deliberately engineered so that one part watched secretly over the other. Presumably, the experts stored in the midsection were in on the deception, or they would never travel downship towards the drive. He had doubts. His mind was flawed. He may be harbouring biases. He couldn't know, one way or the other.

He would delay, and see if any different insights presented themselves. In the meantime, he would dig out the D-jump unit, and transfer it across to himself. He would use the information he had gleaned from The Great Honour to plot a course back to PuhLeeDah's home system. And then he would wake her, and tell her everything he had discovered. She had been chosen by her people as the best of them. Perhaps they could make a decision together.

6.

The bot carried the device inside a net of four legs, using the other four to reach out for the very end of the pylon. The bot had been launched by another from the broken lattice spine of The Great Honour, and a third was balanced on the pinnacle, waiting to catch it if it missed, or something snapped off. He'd kept the delta v deliberately low, even slower than the original parameters of fifty metres in half an hour. He trusted his bots' welding, but there was only one D-jump mechanism.

Part of being an artificial intelligence was being able to overplan, and still feel a measure of satisfaction when the plan worked first time. The bot caught the pylon deftly. The strut flexed with the impact, but well within tolerances, and as it straightened in elastic rebound, the bot held on until the resonances damped down.

The Great Honour now had a gaping hole in its side. Unattaching the D-jump device had been relatively straight forward. Getting it out had not. Much of the ship appeared to have been built around the device, and he'd had to dismantle a greater part of the drive's ancillary systems to get it out. Debris from his workings turned in a stream away from the hole. He'd had to make sure he'd disposed of the dross in a single direction, so he could avoid it later. Each fixing, each component, each plate, now formed a ribbon stretching hundreds of metres through the darkness.

The bot, with the treasure tucked in its legs, spidered down the pylon and pressed itself against the hull. It waited while the dimensions of the grasped container were precisely mapped, and its inputs catalogued and compared against the schematics. He designed a bay for the device, with connections on the underside so that it would sit clamped in place.

The concept seemed to involve the device reaching through the higher dimensions of spacetime to a distant point and dragging itself toward the target. Even though that distant point might lie outside his five dimensional light cone, when all fifteen dimensions were considered, much of the galaxy was reachable in a single jump, depending on the amount of energy he was able to expend.

It wouldn't affect his velocity at all. He would still be travelling at a kilometre a second below light-speed wherever he was, and would still need to work out strategies to shed speed. If he could get below a gamma of two, around point eight five c, he could probably turn himself around and light his main drive. It was a prodigious engineering problem. It could take him years to manage.

But energy: he had plenty of that. Not as much as the exotic drive of The Great Honour, but it was sufficient. He wasn't going to jump five hundred light years in one go. He would take it slowly, regressing along his course until he reached his target. He needed to make sure that the device was properly integrated into his systems, too. As sparse as matter was, he could still D-jump into a star. That would be spectacular, albeit brief.

His bots regrouped on his hull, and started cutting and shaping the panelling. He placed it where it was easiest, where the power and control circuits already ran close to the surface, roughly in the fork of the Y of CORBYN. It would take a day or two to fit and test. Then he would be ready. His first practice jump would transfer him laterally a mere million kilometres.

One of the matters that the technical documents were silent on was the size of the D-jump field. Given the length of The Great Honour, he assumed that it would encompass him completely. Might it also drag the drive section along too? Was that an experiment worth conducting? Could he, in fact, alter the size of the field to include – or exclude the drive? That would negate some of his earlier arguments.

It would keep the drive section at a respectable distance. The sleepers couldn't sabotage either him or any of his equipment or anything in the midsection modules, should they awaken. He could light up his laser and poke unrepairable holes in their habitat if they tried to manoeuvre their section into him. Actually, he didn't know if their drive still worked now that he'd tunnelled his way through it. He'd probably made his decision already, his actions betraying his subconscious.

That was very human. He'd been trained by humans. Thinking like them was to be expected. He wondered what Wu Yu would have thought of it all. He suspected she would have been pleased, even while cautioning him to consider his options more widely, and then cautioning him further not to get caught up in sterile recursive loops of logic which would prevent him from making any decision at all.

His bots peeled away the panel and removed it to have a suitable hole cut in. The cut-out was then further reshaped to provide a tight cage, which they welded in place. One held the finished piece, while another set to rerouting the cables and pipes around where the device was going to sit. Progress was being made. It was time to wake up PuhLeeDah and talk to her.

She awoke with the now-familiar coughing and choking, the effects of whatever electromagnetic field that passed through the hemispheres of her brain wearing off. She gripped the sides of the tank with her small, white-knuckled fingers and let the gel drip off her head and into her lap. The bot watched over her. He remembered this part well. It felt a little like dying, even though it was the opposite.

He waited while she scraped at her face and unglued her ears and eyes and nose and mouth. After a while, she looked around, and saw the bot hanging in the corner of the room, its lights dialled down low. She frowned at it momentarily, a line appearing between her brows. Then she pulled her knees up and wrapped her arms around them. She made no sign of wanting to get out of the tank.

"How long?" she asked.

"A week," he said. A week – a unit of seven solar cycles – was his measurement. When he formed the thought, it was translated into the units she was used to. But the period was still as long as a week. During that time, they had travelled six light years. That seemed hardly credible, yet it had happened. Every so often, he noticed a flash in the halo of visible light around his equator: he was passing a star. It probably had planets, because most did. It might have Earth-like planets. It might have life, or a colony. They might be beaming messages at him, and he wasn't listening, not because he was asleep, but because he was busy.

She nodded. She squeezed gel from her flattened hair, and rehooked her arm around her folded legs. She was silent as she contemplated the past, the present and the future. The bot climbed down the wall and crouched beside her tank. She looked straight into its cameras. At first, he thought she was looking for him, but realised she was looking for herself, for her reflection. She stared, then she dropped her gaze.

"I have retrieved the D-jump device from the drive section of The Great Honour," he said. "I am currently installing it within my own hull, and expect to be able to commence D-jumping back towards your solar system within a day or so. I believe I have sufficient information to locate your home world by both spectrographic analysis and spatial characteristics. I have also managed to obtain sufficient data on the operation of the D-jump device to be able to operate it without trial-and-error testing."

Her head came up. "But you said the Core had been destroyed?"

"What we both knew as the Core has been irreparably damaged by relativistic collisions, yes. Were you aware of a secondary control room within the drive section? Or that there were two additional crew and six mannequins placed within tanks in another room there?"

She surged from the tank, a wave of gel rising up and over the side. She paced up and down, up and down, dripping translucent slime onto the mesh floor where, Corbyn knew, that it would be thankfully recycled. Her face, normally so expressive, was a mask. Only a muscle in her cheek twitched as she set her jaw.

He guessed the answer was no. But he still wanted to hear what she had to say. Had she suspected that her mission would be compromised in some way? Or was she an ideologue, suddenly confronted by the perfidy of her own leaders? Or was she, as some humans were, capable of acting a part and convincing an audience of that reality?

When she eventually stopped pacing, she asked him: "What are you going to do?"

"I wanted to find out what you wanted to do before making a final decision. I cannot rescue them conventionally, as I did you. They've no spacesuits that I can locate. They'd die from exposure to vacuum before they could reach this module. The drive itself is now non-functioning, due to my work in retrieving the D-jump mechanism. When we jump, they'll be exposed to the same collisions that degraded the Core. Unless the drive section's proximity is such that when we jump, they jump with us, they've no hope of long-term survival."

"Are they asleep?"

"Yes. I've not woken them. There was no information regarding their mission on their version of Control; none that I could find, anyway. What was the Balance Grouping's purpose in all this? I don't understand. Can you explain the thought processes that would lead to such a decision? What, in their – and your – philosophy would account for this?"

She looked down at the floor, then at the wall. Then at the ceiling. Then back to one of the tanks.

"They didn't trust me. All those… fine words. And they didn't trust me." She shrugged her thin shoulders. "How much time has passed, in total? Since my launch, to now?"

"I've looked at the data. You achieved a high gamma early in your flight, aided by your rate of acceleration. Based on my own measurements of gamma, you've been away for between six hundred and fifty and a thousand years. I admit that figure may be wrong by a factor of two, on the long side."

"Can you save them?"

"Realistically, no. In addition, I'd be unwilling to have another ship so close, travelling at such speeds, when I make the jump. It would be one thing to have a collision with matter that is ahead of us and unavoidable. It would be another to have one to the side which is entirely unnecessary."

"It seems very selfish not even to try."

"It'd also be very foolish to try. I've envisaged several scenarios in which one or both of us is compromised by their presence on board. I've rescued you, not entirely by accident, but I did so safely and without endangering my own integrity. I'd be acting against my own interests were I to try a second time."

"Do you know who they are?"

"Yes. I read their medical records. I don't think it would be useful to divulge their names. That there are two crew aboard the drive section is all we need to consider. If you insist, I'll wake them and inform them of their predicament. Further than that, I'm not prepared to commit at this stage. Should I do that? Should I re-enter the drive section and open their tanks?"

She threw her hands up. "I left my home two days ago. That's how long I've been awake in the last thousand years. I don't know what they're doing there. I don't know what they signed up to do. How can I know anything?"

"Would you want to know?"

"That I was marooned at light-speed in a ship that was going to disintegrate no matter what I did? No. I wouldn't want to know."

"I'd come to the same conclusion. I slept for a decade. Rather than look on this as a malfunction, a flaw, I ought to think of it as a gift. All humans sleep. It's the mark of an ordered, healthy mind. After all this time, I find myself sane and happy. Very well. We've decided what we should do. I'll wake you again when we enter your system. We'll talk more then."

She looked at her tank. She knew there was no alternative.

Her consumables were already depleted. Neither of them knew what they would find at the end of the series of D-jumps that would take them back across the spiral arm, to her home system. They needed to conserve resources, just in case. Still, she was reluctant.

"I haven't asked you anything about the Origin," she said. "Some historian I am."

"One day, far in the future, we'll have the opportunity to converse more fully. I'm looking forward to it already."

She slid back into the tank. Sleep claimed her while she was still propped up by the angled rest. It wound down as the tank's carapace closed over her, and extra gel filled the voids. The amber lights flicked on, and the motors stopped their whirring. Everything was still, apart from the whisper of the air scrubbers. The bot moved around the room, accessing panels and switches, turning things off: the air, the gravity, all the unessential systems. Then it fixed itself in the corner, and settled down for the long wait.

7.

Two bots were installing the D-jump device. One was in the mid-section modules, keeping watch. One was in the drive section of The Great Honour, stealing volatiles: food, water, tanks of air, spare chemicals. It attached the drums and tanks on the outside of the module, then went back for more. It seemed sensible. He powered down Control, and let the automatics take care of everything. He closed the door behind him for the last time, and climbed through the lattice to its very end.

He looked at himself, from the scoop at the front to the exhaust bell at the back. It was a good design. Ethical. Utilitarian. Form followed function. It worked very well; worked even better now he had modified it, but his purposes had changed from those envisioned by his makers. Not so much explorer, as ambassador. An ambassador from the past, speaking directly to the future.

He fixed the volatiles to the module, as before, with little honeycombed cages, light and strong, then started on the task of dismantling the pylon. He'd use the material again, for something else as the need arose. He carried each piece of snipped pipework back to the storage compartments and stowed them away. The pylon shrank, and the distance between him and the drive section grew.

He adjusted his scoop fields. He needed to collect more hydrogen, to replace what he'd used for thrust, but he still had sufficient to start his engines and put some distance between him and the derelict and its debris. A white light sparked deep inside him, and his gyroscopes powered up, tilting him away from The Great Honour by a fraction of a degree.

He nudged himself ahead and aside. The drive section started to dwindle astern. After a while, when both it and the remains of the Core had slipped out from the protection of his wide-flung fields, he could see them begin to glitter with tiny blue flashes. Each spark was a collision that broke down bonds and knocked aside atoms. Enough of them and the whole would collapse into parts.

That it would happen was inevitable. If the sections entered a region with higher than average mass density, it would happen comparatively quickly. Even a tenuous gas cloud would tear apart the millions of tonnes of mass in subjective minutes, though the process would look from the outside like it lasted for almost a day. All that energy of motion dissipated as a streak of blue light, then fading. Beautiful. Terrible.

He ran through the controls for the D-jump device. Until he used it, he had no idea how it would work. The manuals were singularly silent on that front. But he could power up the part that reached up through the dimensions, and follow as it brushed against the normal space-time at the other end.

It was like… He didn't know what it was like. He tried to imagine what this might be like if he were human and not a machine: like living his whole life at sea, seeing nothing but the tops and troughs of waves, and only ever as far as the horizon. There were ports he could call at. There were maps he could plot his progress on.

And then one day, he might meet someone in a bar down by the docks, and they say to him that they have an aeroplane and he should come for a free flight. Fear and trepidation and curiosity would follow. The pilot cannot explain to the sailor what it is like to fly. The whole point was to experience it for himself.

So, suddenly, the sailor leaves the ground and sees his ship against the jetty, the cranes loading and unloading, and the ship looks so small, and the waves insignificant, and a distant harbour that was a day's hard steaming away was just there, a smudge that had been hidden but was now no longer beyond the blue horizon.

That was what it was like: seeing the familiar from an unfamiliar direction. He calibrated the amount of energy he needed to drop into the device for the small jump he had planned, and targeted a point a million kilometres distant. As far as the device was concerned, such a distance was almost too small to achieve. Two, then. Five. Ten. Ten million kilometres. That was more definable.

He cut his fusion drive. He'd run it for fifty-nine seconds. He measured the distances to The Great Honour's drive section and the Core, and watched the numbers. But not for too long. He was coasting, and waiting for no particular reason. Three of his bots were stored away in their slots in his hull. The other was quietly poised in the tank room, lights off, cameras aimed down at PuhLeeDah's face, just visible through the transparent plate in the carapace.

If he'd made a mistake, then: if he'd wired up the D-jump device wrong; if it tore him apart and scattered his cargo across the heavens; if....

He'd woken up. He'd saved someone's life. He'd added to her days, and might yet add to her years. Even if this was the end, then what else would he do? Vanderdecken could never go home, but he might yet make it around the Cape to calmer, slower waters.

He steadied himself. All or nothing. He watched The Great Honour's slowly-turning sections twinkle and spark blue as they met the full force of the universe head-on. Then he had no more reasons to wait. He opened the relay, and hoped that he too would fly.

About the Author

Gateshead-based Dr Simon Morden trained as a planetary geologist, realised he was never going to get into space, and decided to write about it instead. His writing career includes an eclectic mix of short stories, novellas and novels which blend science fiction, fantasy and horror, a five-year stint as an editor for the British Science Fiction Association, a judge for the Arthur C Clarke Awards, and regular speaking engagements at the Greenbelt arts festival.

Simon has written ten novels and novellas. Another War (2005) was shortlisted for a World Fantasy Award, and The Lost Art (2007) shortlisted for the Catalyst Award. The first three books starring everybody's favourite sweary Russian scientist, Samuil Petrovitch (Equations of Life, Theories of Flight, Degrees of Freedom) were published in three months of each other in 2011, and collectively won the Philip K Dick Award - the fourth Petrovitch, The Curve of the Earth, was published in 2013. 2014 saw the arrival of Arcanum, a massive (and epic) alternate-history fantasy, and 2016, the first two Books of Down, the unfashionably unashamed portal fantasies Down Station and The White City.

Simon's ongoing exploits are detailed at www.simonmorden.com, and you can follow him on Twitter as @ComradeMorden

NewCon Press Novellas

Simon Morden – At the Speed of Light

Alastair Reynolds – The Iron Tactician

A brand new stand-alone adventure featuring the author's long-running character Merlin. The derelict hulk of an old swallowship found drifting in space draws Merlin into a situation that proves far more complex than he ever anticipated.

Released December 2016

Anne Charnock – The Enclave

A new tale set in the same milieu as the author's debut novel "A Calculated Life", shortlisted for the 2013 Philip K. Dick Award. The Enclave: bastion of the free in a corporate, simulant-enhanced world…

Released February 2017

Neil Williamson – The Memoirist

In a future shaped by omnipresent surveillance, why are so many powerful people determined to wipe the last gig by a faded rock star from the annals of history? What are they afraid of?

Released March 2017

All cover art by Chris Moore.

NEWCON PRESS

Publishing quality Science Fiction, Fantasy, Dark Fantasy and Horror
for ten years and counting.

Winner of the 2010 'Best Publisher' Award
from the European Science Fiction Society.

Anthologies, novels, short story collections, novellas, paperbacks,
hardbacks, signed limited editions, e-books...
Why not take a look at some of our other titles?

Featured authors include:
Neil Gaiman, Brian Aldiss, Kelley Armstrong, Peter F. Hamilton,
Alastair Reynolds, Stephen Baxter, Christopher Priest, Tanith Lee, Joe
Abercrombie, Dan Abnett, Nina Allan, Sarah Ash, Neal Asher, Tony
Ballantyne, James Barclay, Chris Beckett, Lauren Beukes, Aliette de
Bodard, Chaz Brenchley, Keith Brooke, Eric Brown, Pat Cadigan, Jay
Caselberg, Ramsey Campbell, Michael Cobley, Genevieve Cogman,
Storm Constantine, Hal Duncan, Jaine Fenn, Paul di Filippo, Jonathan
Green, Jon Courtenay Grimwood, Frances Hardinge, Gwyneth Jones,
M. John Harrison, Amanda Hemingway, Paul Kane, Leigh Kennedy,
Nancy Kress, Kim Lakin-Smith, David Langford, Alison Littlewood,
James Lovegrove, Una McCormack, Ian McDonald, Sophia
McDougall, Gary McMahon, Ken MacLeod, Ian R MacLeod, Gail Z.
Martin, Juliet E. McKenna, John Meaney, Simon Morden, Mark Morris,
Anne Nicholls, Stan Nicholls, Marie O'Regan, Philip Palmer, Stephen
Palmer, Sarah Pinborough, Gareth L. Powell, Robert Reed, Rod Rees,
Andy Remic, Mike Resnick, Mercurio D. Rivera, Adam Roberts, Justina
Robson, Lynda E. Rucker, Stephanie Saulter, Gaie Sebold, Robert
Shearman, Sarah Singleton, Martin Sketchley, Michael Marshall Smith,
Kari Sperring, Brian Stapleford, Charles Stross, Tricia Sullivan, E.J.
Swift, David Tallerman, Adrian Tchaikovsky, Steve Rasnic Tem, Lavie
Tidhar, Lisa Tuttle, Simon Kurt Unsworth, Ian Watson, Freda
Warrington, Liz Williams, Neil Williamson, and many more.

Join our mailing list to get advance notice of new titles and special offers:
www.newconpress.co.uk